Frederick Young

A Winter Tour in South Africa

Frederick Young

A Winter Tour in South Africa

ISBN/EAN: 9783337123109

Printed in Europe, USA, Canada, Australia, Japan

Cover: Foto ©Andreas Hilbeck / pixelio.de

More available books at **www.hansebooks.com**

MY WAGON.

A

WINTER TOUR

IN

SOUTH AFRICA

BY

SIR FREDERICK YOUNG, K.C.M.G.

(Reprinted by permission from the Proceedings of the Royal Colonial Institute, with large additions, Illustrations, and a Map.)

LONDON:

E. A. PETHERICK & CO.,
33, PATERNOSTER ROW, E.C.

1890.

To

HER ROYAL HIGHNESS, PRINCESS LOUISE,

MARCHIONESS OF LORNE,

This Volume, describing a recent tour, during which
a large portion of Her Majesty's magnificent
Dominions in South Africa were traversed,
is, by gracious permission, dedicated
with feelings of sincere
respect.

INTRODUCTION.

THE growth of the great Colonies of the British Empire is so phenomenal, and their development is so rapid, and remarkable, that if we are to possess a correct knowledge of their actual state, and condition, from year to year, their current history requires to be constantly re-written.

The writer of a decade since, is, to-day, almost obsolete. He has only produced a current record of facts, and places, at the period he wrote. This is especially the case with South Africa.

I have recently returned from a very interesting tour in that remarkable country. My impressions were noted down, as they occurred, from day to day. A summary of my observations,

and of the incidents, in connection with my
journey, was the subject of a Paper I read
at the opening meeting of the present Session
of the Royal Colonial Institute, on the 12th
of November last.   I wish it to be understood
that the opinions expressed on that occasion
were my own, and that the Institute as a
body is in no way responsible for them.   This
Paper has formed the outline of the volume,
which—with much new matter from my note
book—I now offer to the public, in the belief,
that the narrative of a traveller, simply seeking
instruction, as well as amusement, from a few
months tour, while traversing some 12,000 miles
by sea, and 4,000 miles by land, through the
wonderful country in which he lately roamed,
might prove of some use, in awakening addi-
tional interest on the part of the general public,
to one of the most promising, and valuable
portions of the Colonial Empire.

In this spirit, I offer my "Winter Tour in South Africa," to my countrymen, "at home and beyond the seas," in the hope that it may receive from them, a favourable reception.

On the "Political Situation," I have spoken strongly and frankly, I hope not too much so. The result of my personal observations has convinced me, that I have only correctly expressed the opinions, very widely entertained by large classes of Her Majesty's subjects in South Africa.

I cannot conclude without acknowledging the aid I have derived from the Statistical information contained in the "Argus Annual," and it also affords me much pleasure to thank Mr. James R. Boosé, the Librarian of the Royal Colonial Institute, for the assistance he has rendered me.

FREDERICK YOUNG.

5, Queensberry Place, S.W.
1st *January*, 1890.

LIST OF ILLUSTRATIONS.

CONTENTS.

CONTENTS

THE VOYAGE.

On the 3rd of May last, I left Southampton in the s.s. *Spartan* for Cape Town. This three weeks' ocean voyage has become one of the most enjoyable it is possible to take by those who are seeking health or pleasure on the sea. The steamers of the great companies, which carry on so admirably the weekly communication between England and South Africa, are so powerful, handsome, and commodious, their captains and crews are so attentive and obliging, their food and cabin accommodation so ample and luxurious, that it seems impossible for anyone, excepting a confirmed grumbler, to find any reasonable fault with any of their arrangements, where all are so good. Passengers will select the particular vessel by which they desire to travel, rather by the convenience of the date fixed for sailing, than from any particular choice of the name of the steamer, either belonging to the Castle Mail Packet Company, the Union Steamship Company, or any other line.

A sea voyage of the kind I have recently taken does not give opportunity for much striking incident, or exciting variety. If restful and pleasant to those who are escaping for a while from the bustle and turmoil of life on shore, it is at all events bound to be somewhat monotonous, in spite of the many amusements which are daily arranged, including cricket, tennis, quoits, concerts, dances, etc., of which I experienced a fair share. On many occasions I was called upon to preside at concerts, lectures, etc., not only amongst the saloon passengers, but also in the third class cabin. A rough voyage across the Bay of Biscay, a view of the Tagus, a brief run on shore to look at the picturesque capital of Portugal, a gaze at the spot, which marks the memory of the scene of the fearful earthquake of 1755, which destroyed most of the town, and 50,000 of its inhabitants ; a short stay at the lovely island of Madeira, sufficient to glance at its beautiful scenery, to breathe its balmy air, to taste its delicious fruits, and to land at its pretty town of Funchal, to see some of its charming surroundings ; a passing peep at Teneriffe, which is now receiving so much attention in Europe as an attractive health resort ; a few days' run of exhausting heat through the tropics ; a visit to Saint Helena, enough to allow of a drive to Longwood, and a look at the room, where the first Napoleon

breathed his last—leaving there the legacy of the
shadow of a mighty name to all time—on this
"lonely rock in the Atlantic"; a few days more
of solitary sailing over a stormy sea, a daily
look-out for whales, porpoises, dolphins, flying
fish, sharks, and albatrosses; a glance upward,
night after night, into the starry sky, to gaze
on the Southern Cross, so much belauded, and
yet so disappointing in its appearance, after
the extravagant encomiums lavished on it; and
at length, on the early morning of May 24, I
safely reached Cape Town.

CAPE TOWN.

To produce the most favourable impression of any new place, it is essential that it should be seen for the first time in fine weather. Places look so very different under a canopy of cloud, and, perhaps, a deluge of rain, or when they are bathed in the sunshine of a beautiful day. Happily for me, my first view of Cape Town was under the latter genial aspect. I need scarcely say, that I was, in consequence, quite charmed with my first sight of this celebrated town, the seat of Government of the Cape Colony. What made the scene more than usually striking to a traveller, fresh from the

sea, was, that it was the Queen's birthday, and
the day dawned with a most perfect specimen
of "Queen's weather." Cape Town was literally
en fête. The inhabitants thronged the streets.
I was astonished at the great 'variety of gay
costumes among the motley crowd—English,
Dutch, Germans and French, Malays, Indian
Coolies, Kafirs, and Hottentots—a tremendous
gathering, in fact, of all nations, and "all
sorts and conditions of men." There was a
grand review of all the military branches of
the Service, in which His Excellency the
Administrator, General Smyth, surrounded by
a brilliant staff, received the homage due to
the British flag; and, as her representative on
this occasion, to Her Majesty's honoured name.
The review was followed by a regatta in the
afternoon. It was quite refreshing to a new
arrival, like myself, to observe the enthusiastic
evidences of loyal feeling everywhere exhibited

GOVERNMENT HOUSE, CAPE TOWN.

in the capital of the Colony to our Queen, the beloved and venerated head of the British Empire.

Before commencing my long and interesting tour "up country," I spent a few most pleasant days at Cape Town. My impressions of it, and of its beautiful surroundings, could not fail to be most favourable. The panoramic view of its approach from Table Bay, at the foot of Table Mountain, is very fine. The town itself appeared to me much cleaner, and brighter than I expected to see it, although, it must be admitted, there is still considerable room for improvement in its sanitary arrangements, and also in the accommodation, and condition of its hotels, to make them as attractive as they ought to be. The best of them do not come at all up to our standard at home, nor to our English ideas of comfort and convenience. A great improvement in these respects, I am satisfied, is not only necessary, but would pay well, and induce a far larger number of visitors to stay at Cape Town, and avail themselves of its attractions of climate, and fine surroundings.

While I was at Cape Town, I visited among other places, the House of Parliament, the Observatory, the South African Museum, the Public Library, the Botanic Gardens, &c.

The House of Parliament, which was opened for public use in 1885, is a very handsome building, having a frontage of 264 feet, and is divided into a central portico, leading into the grand vestibule, the two debating chambers, and side pavilions. The portico, which is of massive dimensions, is approached by a commanding flight of granite steps, which runs round three sides of it. The pavilions are relieved by groups of pilasters with Corinthian capitals, and are surmounted by domes and

PARLIAMENT HOUSE, CAPE TOWN.

ventilators. The whole of the ground floor up to the level of the main floor has been built of Paarl granite, which is obtained from the neighbouring district of that name. The upper part of the building is of red brick, relieved by pilasters and window dressing of Portland cement, the effect being very pleasing to the eye. The interior accommodation for the business of the two Legislative bodies is most complete, and arranged with a careful view to comfort and convenience. In addition to the Debating Chambers, which are sixty-seven feet in length by thirty-six feet in width, there is a lofty hall of stately appearance, with marble pillars, and tesselated pavement, which forms the central lobby, or grand vestibule. I might mention, that the debating chambers are only ten feet in length and width less than the British House of Commons. Adjoining the central lobby is the parliamentary library, a

large apartment, with galleries above each other
reaching to the full height of the building.
The usual refreshment, luncheon, and smoking
rooms have not been forgotten, in connection
with the comfort of the members. The public
are accommodated in roomy galleries, and
ample provision has been made for ladies,
distinguished visitors, and the press. The
portrait of Her Majesty, and the Mace at the
table reminds one forcibly of the fact that one
is still in a portion of the British Empire.
The total cost of the building, including
furniture, was £220,000.

I attended two or three debates in the
House of Parliament, and was much impressed
with the manner in which, in this superb and
commodious legislative chamber, the discussions
were carried on. There was a quiet dignity of
debate, as well as business-like capacity and
orderly tone, observed on both sides of the House,

which might be copied with advantage, as it is in striking contrast to much of the practice, in the Parliament of Great Britain. It is certainly satisfactory to notice, that the modern manners and customs, in the popular branch of our own ancient national assembly, which so frequently fail in orthodox propriety, have not been imitated in the Cape Colony.

At the Record Office attached to the House of Parliament, I went into the vaults, and inspected the early manuscripts of the Dutch, during their original occupation of the Cape of Good Hope. These are most deeply and historically interesting, and valuable. The minute accuracy, with which every incident is recorded is most remarkable. There are bays in these vaults, filled with records, which must be of priceless value to an historical student, and they are now in course of arrangement by the able librarian, Mr. H. C. V.

Leibbrandt, who is the author of a most interesting work entitled "Rambles through the Archives of the Colony of the Cape of Good Hope."*

At the South African Museum I found a valuable collection of beasts, birds, fishes, &c., not only from South Africa, but from various parts of the world. The collection has been enriched by valuable contributions from Mr. Selous, the distinguished African traveller, and sportsman, his donations consisting chiefly of big game, including two gigantic elands, (male and female), buffaloes, antelopes, &c. The series of birds comprises the large number of two thousand species.

A visit of great interest to me was to the South African Public Library, which boasts of about 50,000 volumes, and embraces every branch of science and literature. It contains

---

* The First Series was published in 1887.

three distinct collections, viz., the Dessinian, the
Grey, and the Porter. The first-named was
bequeathed to the Colony in 1761 by Mr.
Joachim Nicholas Von Dessin, and consists of
books, manuscripts and paintings. The Porter
collection took its name from the Hon. William
Porter, and was purchased from the subscriptions
raised for the purpose of procuring a life-size
portrait of that gentleman, in recognition of his
services to the Colony. As, however, Mr. Porter
declined to sit for his portrait, the amount sub-
scribed was appropriated to the purchase of
standard works, to be known as the Porter
Collection. By far the most valuable, however,
is the Grey Collection, numbering about 5,000
volumes, and occupying a separate room. These
were presented by Sir George Grey, Governor
of the Cape Colony from 1854 to 1859, and
still an active member of the New Zealand
House of Representatives. Here are many rare

manuscripts, mostly on vellum or parchment, some of them of the tenth century, in addition to a unique collection of works relating to South Africa generally.

Among the places of worship in Cape Town the most important are St. George's Cathedral, which was built in 1830, and is of Grecian style of architecture, and accomodates about 1,200 persons; and the Dutch Reformed Church, which possesses accomodation for 3,000 persons, and is not unappropriately named the Colonial Westminster Abbey. Beneath its floors lie buried eight Governors of the Colony, the last one being Ryk Tulbagh, who was buried in 1771.

No account of Cape Town would be complete without a reference to the important Harbour Works, and Breakwater, which at once attract the attention of the visitor, and which have been in course of erection for several years past, from the designs of Sir John Coode. These works have been of the greatest importance in extending, and developing the commercial advantages of the port. The Graving Dock now named the Robinson, after the late Governor, Sir Hercules Robinson, was formally opened during the year 1882, and it so happened that the first vessel to enter it was the *Athenian*, in which I returned to England, at the termination of my tour. The whole of the works connected with the building of the Docks and Breakwater reflect credit upon all who have in any way been engaged upon their construction. The amount expended on them up to the end of 1887 was £1,298,103.

Before leaving Cape Town, at the invitation of the Naval Commander-in-Chief, Admiral Wells, I paid a visit to Simon's Town, the chief naval station of the colony. The railway runs at present as far as Kalk Bay, which takes about an hour to get to from Cape Town. Kalk Bay is a pleasant seaside resort for the inhabitants of the colony, the air being regarded as particularly invigorating. The remaining distance of six miles to Simon's Town is performed in a Cape cart, which is a most comfortable vehicle on two wheels, drawn by two horses with a pole between them, and covered with a hood, as a protection from the weather. The scenery from the Kalk Bay station to Simon's Town is very picturesque. A bold sea stretches out on one side of the road, and the mountain on the other. Amongst other things which attracted my attention at Simon's Town was the Dockyard, which embraces about a mile of the foreshore, and contains appliances for repairing modern war vessels, a repairing and victualling depôt, and a patent slip, capable of lifting vessels of about

900 tons displacement. I went with the Admiral, and a party of ladies to have luncheon on board the Steam Corvette *Archer.*

Simon's Bay is very sheltered, excepting from the south-east, with good holding anchorage ground. It seems a quiet, secluded spot, well-adapted for a naval station in this part of the world, although I have heard that an opinion prevails that the fleet should be at Cape Town instead of Simon's Bay. The *Raleigh* is the flag-ship; I saw also some other vessels of the Royal Navy at anchor in the bay. The fortifications which are now in progress for the protection of this important point in our chain of defences will, when completed, render the place practically impregnable from sea attack.

Some of the most beautiful coast scenery I have ever seen is to be found in that very lovely drive by Sea Point to Hout's Bay, and thence back to Cape Town by Constantia and

C

Wynberg. This is a celebrated excursion, and well deserves the praises bestowed upon it. The road has been admirably constructed by convict labour.

A very convenient short line of railway also brings within easy reach of the inhabitants of Cape Town the pretty villages of Mowbray, Rondebosch, Rosebank, Newlands, Wynberg, Constantia, &c., where, in charming villas and other residences, so many of the wealthier classes reside. At Constantia the principal wine farms are situated, the most noted being the Groot Constantia (the Government farm) and High Constantia. Constantia wine can only be produced on these farms. Another farm in this neighbourhood is Witteboomen, which is particularly noted for its peaches, there being over one thousand trees on the farm, in addition to many other kinds of fruit, Another one, and probably the largest in the district, is named "Sillery." Here not many years ago the ground was a wilderness, but it has now attained a high state of perfection, there being at least 140,000 vines and hundreds of fruit trees of all kinds, under cultivation.

At Cape Town I received the first proofs of the kind and lavish attentions which everywhere in South Africa were subsequently bestowed upon me. From everyone, without exception—from His Excellency the Administrator and Mrs. Smyth, and the members of his staff—from all the public men and high officials—from members of the Cape Government, and from the leaders of the Opposition, besides from innumerable private friends, Dutch and English alike, I received such cordial tokens of goodwill, that I can only express my deep sense of appreciation of their most genial and friendly hospitality. I bid adieu to Cape Town (which I was visiting for the first time

in my life) with the conviction that I was
truly in a land, not of strangers, but of real
friends, who desired to do everything in their
power to make my visit to South Africa
pleasant and agreeable to me ; and this
impression I carried with me ever afterwards
at every place I visited during the whole
of my tour.

On Wednesday, May 29, I left Cape Town
at 6.30 p.m. for Kimberley, passing Beaufort
West, the centre of an extensive pastoral
district, and De Aar, the railway junction
from Cape Town and Port Elizabeth. This
journey is a long one, of between 600 and
700 miles, and of some forty-two hours by
railway. I travelled all through that night,
and the whole of the next day, through the
most remarkable kind of country I ever saw.
Flat, and apparently as level, as a bowling-
green (although we were continually rising from

our starting-point at Cape Town to a height
at Kimberley of about 3,800 feet above the
sea), a sandy and dreary desert, with occasionally low, and barren hills in the far distance—
not a tree to be seen, and scarcely any vestige
of vegetation, excepting now and then, a few
of the indigenous Mimosa shrubs, which, for
hundreds of miles, grow fitfully on this desolate
soil. This is the wonderful tract of country
called the Great Karoo. Not a sign of animal
life is to be detected, at this period of the
year. During the summer months it affords
pasturage for large flocks of sheep. It is a
vast interminable *sea of lone land*, over which
the eye wanders unceasingly during the whole
of the daylight hours.

KIMBERLEY.

AFTER another long night in the railway train, at noon on the second day, after leaving Cape Town, I reached the celebrated diamond town of Kimberley, the population of which consists of about 6,000 Europeans, with a native population estimated at about 10,000, chiefly concentrated in the mining area.

On my arrival at the railway station, I was met by the Mayor, and a deputation of the residents of the town. At a conversazione held later, and which was attended by over four hundred ladies and gentlemen, the following address was presented to me by the

Fellows of the Royal Colonial Institute resident at Kimberley and Beaconsfield :—

"Kimberley, *June* 1st, 1889.

"To Sir Frederick Young, K.C.M.G.

"A Vice-President of the Royal Colonial Institute.

"Dear Sir,—We, the Fellows of the Royal Colonial Institute, resident in the towns and mining centres of Kimberley, and Beaconsfield, South Africa, cordially welcome your arrival amongst us.

"We are persuaded that your visit to this distant part of Her Majesty's Dominions has been undertaken, not merely for personal pleasure, but also on behalf of the great and growing need for the consolidation and expansion of colonial interests throughout the Empire.

"We feel that your own career has been an important factor in the formation of a sound public opinion on this subject, and that it is largely through your patient and far-seeing efforts, that the Royal Colonial Institute has attained its present proud position amongst the various influences, moulding, organising, and guiding the life and destinies of Her Majesty's Colonial Empire.

" We believe the present time to be vitally important in the history of Her Majesty's Dominions in South Africa. The tide of confederation, and corporate union is manifestly rising, the wave of extended British influence is flowing northwards, the various nationalities and states of this vast country are educating themselves by experience to see the folly and sterile weakness of isolation, and are learning to realise the inherent strength, and vitality of mutual co-operation, based on a self respecting, yet unselfish responsibility to South Africa as a whole.

" We venture to suggest that this growing

feeling for co-operation will prove a valuable element in the growth, and formation in the near future, of one Grand Confederation of all countries and peoples, owing allegiance to, or claiming corporate alliance with, Her Britannic Majesty's Empire.

"We rejoice, as members of the Royal Colonial Institute, that your personal merits and public career have been recognised by Her Majesty in the honour conferred upon you, which we trust you will enjoy for many years.

"Coming amongst us as a Vice-President of our own Institute, your presence symbolises to us the aspiration, radiant in hope, and prophetic in promise, which animates all true and loyal subjects of Her Majesty, and which is alone worthy of our past history, and present re-sponsibilities—the aspirations of a strong and united people for a vigorous, and progressive ' United Empire.'"

To anyone visiting, for the first time, this
great centre of the diamond industry of South
Africa the scene is most extraordinary. The
excitement and bustle, the wild whirl of
vehicular traffic, the fearful dust, the ceaseless
movement of men and women of all descriptions,
and of every shade of complexion and colour,
are positively bewildering. The thoughts of
everybody appear to be centred in diamonds,
and the prevailing talk and speech are accord-
ingly. Being the recipient, myself, of the
most kind attention and genial and generous
hospitality, my stay was most agreeable, and
pleasant. Great facilities were afforded me for
seeing everything connected with this wonderful
industry, and satisfying myself, that there are
no present signs of its being exhausted or
"played out." Indubitable evidences were
given me, that diamonds continue to be found
in as large quantities as ever. They appeared
to me to be "as plentiful as blackberries."

At the Bultfontein Mine I descended to the bottom of the open workings in one of the iron buckets, used for bringing up the "blue ground" to the surface. This is rather a perilous adventure. To go down by a wire rope, some five or six hundred feet perpendicular into the bowels of the earth with lightning rapidity, standing up in an open receptacle, the top of which does not approach your waist, oscillating like a pendulum, while you are holding on "like grim death" by your hands, is something more than a joke. It certainly ought not to be attempted by anyone who does not possess a cool head and tolerable nerve.

Here I saw multitudes of natives employed,— as afterwards in the De Beer's, the Kimberley, and other diamond mines,—with pickaxes, shovels, and other tools, breaking down the ground at the sides of the mine, perched at

various spots, and many a giddy height. Diamond
mining at Kimberley is altogether a very
wonderful specimen of the development of a
new industry. In this mine I had explained
to me the various processes, by which diamonds
are discovered in the rocky strata which is
being constantly dug out of the enormous
circular hole, constituting it.

I also visited the celebrated De Beer's
Mine. This vast mine, where some thousands
of workmen, white and coloured, are employed,
is carried on much in the same way as the
Bultfontein, as far as the different processes are concerned, of treating the material
in which the diamonds are found. It is
much richer, however, in "blue ground," and
consequently far more valuable results are
obtained from it. For instance, the average
value of each truck load of stuff from the
Bultfontein is said to be about 8s., while from

the De Beer's it is 28s. or 30s. The latter
mine is now worked underground, in the same
way as copper and coal mines are worked in
England. Excellent arrangements are made
for the protection and well-being of the
native workmen, especially by the introduction
of "compounds" during the last year or two.
These are vast enclosures, with high walls,
where the natives compulsorily reside, after
their daily work is done during the whole
time they remain at work in the mine. This
system has been attended with the most
satisfactory results. I went over the De Beer's
"compound," where I saw an immense number
of natives, all appearing lively, cheerful, and
happy. A large number were playing at cards
(they are great gamblers), and others amusing
themselves in various ways. No intoxicating
liquor is permitted to be sold within the
"compounds." The weekly receipts for ginger

beer amount to a sum, which seems fabulous, averaging from £60 to £100 a week. The natives can purchase from the " compound " store every possible thing they want, from a tinpot to a blanket, from a suit of old clothes to a pannikin of mealies. Before the establishment of the "compounds," when the natives had the free run of the town, and could obtain alcoholic liquor—on Saturday nights especially, after they had done their work and received their weekly wages—Kimberley was a perfect pandemonium.

An interesting visit was one to the central offices of the United Companies, where I saw the diamonds, as they are prepared ready for sale, lying on a counter in small assorted lots, on white paper. This is a most remarkable sight. The lots, varying from half-a-dozen to twenty, or thirty, or more diamonds, are spread out arranged according to their estimated value. I took up one, which I was told would probably fetch £1,000, and of which there were several similar ones in the different parcels on the counter. The manager showed me a paper of a sale to the buyers, a day or two before, of a parcel, which was calculated to realise £14,189, and which actually was sold afterwards for £14,150 ; showing the surprising accuracy of the previous estimate on the part of the experts.

Another day I went to the Central Kimberley Diamond Mine. After going over the mine, my party and myself all "assisted" at the counter in one of the large sheds in picking out diamonds from the heap of small stones just brought up and laid out from the day's washings. It is rather a fascinating occupation, turning over the heap with a little triangular piece of tin held in one hand, and continually "scraped" along the board. I found several

diamonds. We were told, after we had been
working diligently for an hour or two—there
were six of us—that the value of the diamonds
we had found, and placed in the manager's box,
was probably £1,200. This seemed to us a
good afternoon's work. The entire district of
Kimberley seems to teem with diamonds, and
yet there is no cessation in the demand for
them, and they are still rising in price.
Accidents are frequent at these mines, but
excellent provision for meeting these misfortunes is made in the admirably conducted
Kimberley Hospital (where there are no less than
360 beds for patients), which I visited during
my stay. It is under the management of a
very remarkable woman, Sister Henrietta, and
reflects the greatest credit on everyone connected with its conduct, and support. The
number of native cases treated at the Hospital
during the year 1887 was 2,975.

Kimberley has risen with immense speed, commencing from what is generally known as a "rush," to a large and prosperous centre of wealth, trade, and commerce. There, where only a few years since, was to be found a collection of tents and small huts, I found a city with handsome buildings, churches, stores, institutions, and law courts, and, above all, a well ordered society. Some of the buildings which I might specially mention, are the Town Hall, the Post Office, the High Court, and the Public Library. which has been in existence about seven years, and is superintended with such excellent results and most gratifying success by the Judge President. One noticeable fact connected with this Library is that the number of works of fiction annually taken out by the subscribers, exceeds. per head of the population, that of any Public Library in the United Kingdom.

The Kimberley Waterworks, which I also visited, have proved a great boon to this part of the Colony. They were erected at a cost of £400,000, the water supply being obtained from the Vaal River, seventeen miles away.

After spending a most pleasant and agreeable week there, I left Kimberley at six o'clock on the morning of June 7, in a wagon drawn by eight horses, and accompanied by five friends, for Warrenton, *en route* for Bechuanaland and the Transvaal. This mode of travelling was quite a novelty to me. Although in this journey of altogether three weeks' duration, we occasionally put up at one or two hotels, at some of the towns, and sometimes at the farmhouses on our way, we frequently "camped out" on the open veldt, and, after finishing our evening meal of the rough-and-ready provisions we carried with us, supplemented by the game we shot, we wrapped ourselves in our karosses, and slept for the night under the canopy of the starlit sky. I occupied the wagon, my more juvenile companions lying on the ground beneath it.

This was my first experience of sleeping in the open air in a wagon, and this, too, in the depth of a South African winter.

The town of Warrenton is situated on the banks of the Vaal River, and is forty-three miles north of Kimberley. It is at present an unimportant town, but diamond diggings have been recently opened, and it is a good cattle district. It took its name from Sir Charles Warren. Soon after leaving Warrenton we crossed the Vaal River on a pontoon. Here a trooper of the Mounted Police joined us, who was said to be a very crack shot. He rode a charming and well-bred grey horse, and had two admirably trained pointers with him. He offered me his horse to ride, he taking my place in the wagon. I had a most enjoyable morning's ride on one of the best little hacks I ever mounted, cantering over the veldt in the track of the wagon for about eight or ten miles—through a charming country with a superb view towards Bechuanaland, the veldt being more wooded and picturesque, than I had hitherto seen.

We slept that night at Drake's Farm. Before starting the next morning, I had a long conversation with Mr. Drake. He was born and brought up in London, and was in business with the firm of Moses & Son. of Cheapside, as a traveller. He came out here nine years ago with £10 in his pocket, and travelled up from Port Elizabeth. Mr. Drake is evidently a man of great energy, and perseverance. He has a high opinion of the country, and a great idea of its future. His farm and store

are situated on the borders of Bechuanaland;
but he now wishes he had settled there, even
in preference to where he is. He laughs at
the idea of there being no water. He says
there is plenty to be found at from seventeen
to twenty-five feet below the surface. But
he says it must be dug for. If properly
irrigated, it is his opinion that thousands and
thousands of tons of mealies might be grown.
He is enthusiastic about the beauty of
Bechuanaland, and spoke of having seen parts
of it in which the charms of English scenery
are to be found, and even greater attractions
than in many gentlemen's parks in the Old
Country. His opinion of the climate is very
high. He told me he would on no account
exchange his present location, with its dry,
pure, and bracing air, so healthful, invigorating,
and free, for the chill, and damps, and fogs
of England. Mr. Drake was in England during

the year 1887 (the Jubilee year), but he was glad to get back again to his home on the border of Bechuanaland—a very comfortable one, as I can testify from my own personal experience.

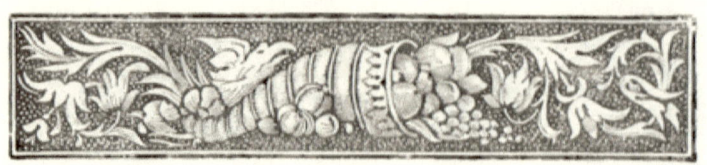

BECHUANALAND.

I WAS very much struck with the appearance of the country on first entering Bechuanaland. The vast plain, over which I was then riding on horseback, was bounded by low, sloping hills, covered with brushwood and trees. It suggested to me forcibly the idea of a "land of promise," wanting only an intelligent and energetic people to secure its proper and successful development.

In fact, as a field for settlement, I entirely concur with the remarks of Mr. John Mackenzie, who has worked for so many years in

Bechuanaland, and who states in his recent
work, entitled, " Austral Africa "—

" I come now to give my own thoughts as
to the capabilities of Bechuanaland as a field
for colonisation. My mind reverts at once to
thrifty, and laborious people who are battling
for dear-life on some small holding in England
or Scotland, and who can barely make ends
meet. I do not think that any class of men,
or men of any colour, endure such hardships
in South Africa. There are portions of
Bechuanaland where, in my opinion, a body
of some hundreds of agricultural emigrants
would, like the Scottish settlers in Baviaan's
river, some sixty years ago, take root from
the first, and make for themselves homes.
If they came in considerable numbers, and
accompanied by a minister of religion, and
possibly a schoolmaster, the children would
not be losers by the change, while the church

and school-house would form that centre in
South Africa, with which all are familiar in
Scotland, and give the people from the first
a feeling of home. I would not suggest that
such men should be merely agriculturists,
but that like most farmers in South Africa
they should follow both branches of farming.
They would begin with some sheep, or angora
goats, and a few cows. In the first instance
they would have a freehold in the village,
with right of pasturage, and they would also
have their farm itself in the neighbourhood,
the size of which would depend upon its
locality and capabilities. But with the milk
of his stock and the produce of his land in
maize, millet and pumpkins, the farmer and
his family would be, from the first, beyond
the reach of want."

For two days more we travelled through
the same kind of country, a fine, bold, and

E

very extensive plain (a promising district for
cattle farming), with rolling and undulating
hills in the distance, till we reached Vryburg,
about a hundred and forty-five miles—in four
days—from Kimberley. This is the capital of
British Bechuanaland, and the head-quarters
of Sir Sidney Shippard, the Administrator.
The town itself contains about 500 inhabitants,
chiefly Europeans. Here we spent four days.
On one of these I was taken by Mr. M——
to visit his fine Bechuanaland farm of 6,000
morgen—12,000 acres—which he has named
"Lochnagar." We left Vryburg at 7.30 a.m.,
and drove about twelve miles in the direction
of Kuruman, reaching Lochnagar Farm about
10 o'clock. While breakfast was preparing,
Mr. M—— took me round the nearest part of
this excellent and valuable farm. He has
had it about three years, and he has already
shown the wonderful capabilities for development

which an enterprising proprietor, possessed of
some capital, can evolve from farms in
Bechuanaland. He first took me into his fruit
garden, which he has stocked with fruits of
all descriptions. I was particularly struck
with the healthy appearance of the wood (it
was then the middle of winter) of the
trees of all sorts of fruit. He has planted
mulberry, apple, pear, apricot, peach, orange,
citron, and several other fruits, all of which
seem to be growing fast, and taking root
vigorously in the soil. A large space is also
devoted to a vineyard, as well as another to
an orchard.

The farm is well irrigated, there being an
abundance of water on it, as I myself saw.
After breakfast we walked round the cattle
lair, where a large portion of his 200 head
of cattle were collected. I was much
impressed with the fine appearance of the

stock. Large-framed, stalwart oxen, and fat
milch cows were round me on every side
during my inspection. I did not notice a
single animal that was not in capital
condition, and fit for the market—if market
there could only be. I next went through a
large enclosure, in which there were about
forty horses, part of the eighty belonging to
Mr. M——. Here I saw several three-year-
olds, and brood mares, and colts, all looking
well and healthy, and containing several good,
well-shaped, and promising specimens of young
horseflesh. Mr. M—— has also a flock of
one thousand sheep on his farm, but these I
did not see, as they were out grazing on the
veldt. We then walked to another portion of
the farm, lying close to the capital house,
built of stone by Mr. M——, to a large
" pan," or lake, in which there were fish
caught with a net. These are a sort of carp,

and a black-coloured fish of seven pounds or eight pounds weight, said to be very good eating. I saw in an outhouse a small collapsible boat, which is sometimes used on the lake. In summer, I am told, the farm looks very pretty, with its long stretches of bright green herbage, and wild flowers, and sunny aspect.

Mr. M—— was born at Cape Town. He is of Dutch origin, and is a fine, stalwart-looking man with great energy of character and keen intelligence. He seems well fitted to be a pioneer farmer, to develop the too-long neglected resources of this fertile land. He is about forty-five years of age, and a bachelor. He first arrived on his farm on a Saturday night three years ago, and the next day commenced tree planting. His first trees were thus planted on a Sunday Morning. This was a good omen of the success he deserves, as I remarked to him.

While I was at Vryburg I was also taken by the proprietor of the Vryburg Hotel to see a farm about five miles off, where they were prospecting for gold. Mr. H—— informed me that the reef I saw, was the same description of rock, I should see at Johannesburg. The people in this neighbourhood are very sanguine; I was told that this may prove a great discovery for Bechuanaland.

KLERKSDORP.

HAVING received the same hospitable attention, as elsewhere, at Vryburg, our wagon party
once more resumed its journey. Thirty miles
brought us to the south-western frontier of the
Transvaal, from whence we travelled on,
through the most dreary, flat, uninteresting,
barren, treeless plain, for two or three days
more, sleeping every night on the veldt, until
we reached Klerksdorp, about 120 miles from
Vryburg. The south-western part of the
Transvaal is certainly exceedingly inferior in
appearance to what I saw in Bechuanaland.

We remained at Klerksdorp three days.
While there I visited one or two of the gold
mines of this promising district.

At the Nooitgedacht Mine I saw the process
performed of pan washing of the previously
crushed quartz. I also went to the stamping
house, where a machine for crushing has been
erected of twenty stamps. I inspected the
mine generally, and its various shafts already
sunk. The work appeared to me to be well
and systematically conducted. Before leaving
this mine the great gold cake lump, weighing
1,370 ozs., which was being forwarded, the day
I was there, to the Paris Exhibition, was put
into my hands. It seemed a wonderfully big
lump of the precious metal, which is so
earnestly sought for by every race of civilised
man.

I also went over another mine, at present in
the early stage of its development, but which

struck me as being conducted, as far as the working management was concerned, on good, sound, business principles—belonging to the Klerksdorp Gold Estates Company.

My stay at Klerksdorp much impressed me with the idea of the future of this town of yesterday's growth. It is only fifteen months ago, (a little more than a year) that the whole of the town on the side of the stream where the Union Hotel is situated, was begun. The inhabitants already number some thousands; and the indications I have seen in the mines, of great prospects of gold being found in large and payable quantities, are very strong. Klerksdorp may yet become a second Johannesburg, whose remarkable and rapid development I was told, would astonish me.

POTCHEFSTROOM.

AFTER leaving Klerksdorp, we travelled the next day in our wagon thirty-two miles, halting for the night at Potchefstroom, which is not only one of the oldest, but one of the most important of the Transvaal districts. Recently the presence of gold-bearing reefs has been demonstrated in many parts of the division. On our way we passed, during the afternoon, a spot on the road where a flock of not less than fifty of those unclean birds, vultures, were hovering over and around the carcase of a recently dead bullock. These

birds are the scavengers of this part of the
world; they feed greedily on carrion, and
rapidly pull a dead animal completely to pieces,
leaving only the bones, which afterwards lie
bleaching on the Veldt, to mark the spot
where it has fallen in death—whether it be
either horse, or mule, or bullock—left to die,
worn out with fatigue by its unfeeling owners.

Before leaving Potchefstroom, the next morning, I paid a hasty visit to the Fort and
Cemetery, rendered so tragically historical in
connection with the Transvaal war. It was
here that my lamented friend, the late
Chevalier Forssman, was shut up with his
family for ninety days, and lost during the
siege, two of his children, a son and a
daughter. I was much struck with the picturesque appearance of Potchefstroom. It has
a population of about 2,000. Another long
two days' journeying of about sixty-four miles,

through a prettier country than the wide
wilderness of the boundless and treeless plain,
we had hitherto passed through in the Western
part of the Transvaal, brought us to Johannesburg.

JOHANNESBURG.

WE had some little trouble in finding our way into the town, as for the last two hours the daylight failed, and we had to grope our way along at a snail's pace in total darkness. This, in a country of such rough roads and deep and dangerous gulleys and water-courses, was a most intricate and difficult proceeding. Eventually, however, we reached our destination about nine o'clock at night.

This "auriferous" town is indeed a marvellous place, lying on the crest of a hill at an elevation of 5,000 feet above the level of

the sea. Along its sides are spread out
every variety of habitation, from the substantial brick and stone structures, which are
being erected with extraordinary rapidity, to
the multitude of galvanised iron dwellings,
and the still not unfrequent tents of the
first, and last comers. It is indeed a wonderful and bewildering sight to view it from the
opposite hill across the intervening valley.
Scarcely more than two years have elapsed
since this town of twenty-five thousand inhabitants commenced its miraculous existence.
The excitement and bustle of the motley
crowd of gold seekers and gold finders is
tremendous. the whole of the live-long day.
The incessant subject of all conversation is
gold, gold, gold. It is in all their thoughts,
excepting, perhaps, a too liberal thought of
drink. The people of Johannesburg think of
gold; they talk of gold: they dream of gold.

I believe, if they could, they would eat and
drink gold. But, demoralising as this is to a
vast number of those, who are in the vortex
of the daily doings of this remarkable place,
the startling fact is only too apparent to
anyone who visits Johannesburg. It is to be
hoped that the day will come when the
legitimate pursuit of wealth will be followed
in a less excitable, and a more calm and
decorous manner, than at present regretably
prevails.

I spent a pleasant, as well as interesting,
week at Johannesburg; and, during my stay,
visited several of the mines, among them
Knight's, the Jumpers, Robinson's, Langlaagte,
&c. At Robinson's, I had an opportunity of
inspecting the wonderful battery just completed, and in full working order, constructed
on the most approved principles for gold
crushing, with sixty head of stamps. It is a

marvellous specimen of mechanical contrivance
for crushing the ore. Many parts of the
machinery work automatically. I ascended
the various floors, and had all the processes
minutely and clearly described to me in a
most courteous manner, by the superintendent
of the battery. I afterwards went down into
the mine, first to the 70-feet, and then again
to the 150-feet levels. In this way, I passed
two hours wandering underground with a
candle in my hand, and inspecting the gold-
bearing lodes of one of the richest mines in
the Randt. This mine possesses magnificent
lodes, and millions of tons of gold-producing
quartz. There is a prospect of most profitable
results in it for years to come. Altogether,
from what I have seen of the various gold
mines of Johannesburg, I am satisfied of the
permanence of its gold fields. Of course they
are not all of equal value; but many, even

JOHANNESBURG MARKET PLACE.

of the poorer mines, when they come to be worked more scientifically, and on proper business principles, will ultimately be found to pay fairly, although they may never be destined to yield such brilliant results, as some of those I have mentioned. The Market Square (of which an illustration is given) is the largest in South Africa, covering an area of 1,300 feet in length, and 3C0 feet in width. Some idea of the growth of Johannesburg may be gathered from the fact, that at the latter part of the year 1886 there was not a Post Office in existence, whilst the revenue of that department for the first quarter of 1887 was £167, and at the end of 1888 it had risen to £7,588.

This extraordinary and rapid growth has unfortunately produced the usual results, when an immense population is suddenly planted on a limited area, without any proper sanitary

G

arrangements being provided for their protection. From its elevated situation and
naturally pure and dry atmosphere, Johannesburg ought to be a very healthy town.
That it notoriously is not so, and that the
amount of sickness and death-rate from fever
and other diseases is abnormal, must, undoubtedly, be attributed to the great neglect
and utter absence of an efficient system of
drainage. I fear this state of things will
continue; and the certainty of serious increase,
as the population continues to grow rapidly,
is only too likely, until there is established
some kind of municipal body, acting under
Governmental authority, to adopt a thorough
and complete system of sanitation. It is to be
hoped that the Transvaal Government, which is
having its treasury so rapidly filled from the
pockets of the British population, which is pour-
ing into Johannesburg, as well as into so many

other towns in the Transvaal, will awake in time to the importance of taking measures for thoroughly remedying this great and glaring evil, which is becoming such a scandal, as well as creating such widely spread and justifiable alarm among the British community in the Transvaal.*

---

* Since my return to England I am glad to hear that a Sanitary Board is to be established at Johannesburg.

PRETORIA.

FROM Johannesburg I proceeded to Pretoria, a distance of about thirty-five miles, through a fine, and bold, and sometimes pretty country. Some of the views on the way were extensive and picturesque. Pretoria itself is an exceedingly pretty town, situated at the base of the surrounding hills. There is a continuous, and most abundant supply of water running through all the principal streets. Here, again, I was forcibly reminded of the absence of any municipal body—although Pretoria is the seat of Government—for dealing with the sanitary and other wants of the town.

The dust, every day (as at Johannesburg), was intolerable, although, with the abundance of water flowing unceasingly through the streets, it would be the easiest thing in the world to apply it, as much as could possibly be wanted, to water them, and keep the dust down. I remained for three weeks at Pretoria. While there I attended some meetings of the Volksraad, accompanied by a Dutch friend who kept me *au fait* of the proceedings by translating to me the speeches of the various members, on the subjects under discussion.

The debates are held in a very large, somewhat low-pitched apartment. About fifty members were present. The President of the Volksraad sat at a table on a platform, covered with green cloth. On one side of him, at the same table, sat Paul Kruger, the President of the Transvaal Republic. General

Joubert—who defeated the English at Majuba Hill—sat at a separate table on the left of the chairman.

I was also present, more than once, at the sittings of the High Court of Justice. The proceedings are conducted both in English and Dutch.

By the courtesy of the Chief Justice, I was introduced by him at a special interview, which lasted half-an-hour, to Paul Kruger. During our conversation, which was carried on by my speaking in English, translated into Dutch by the Chief Justice, I referred to the fact of my having been introduced to him in England some years ago. I went on to speak of my having come from England to South Africa to learn. That I had already learned much, and that I was much pleased with all I had seen, especially in the Transvaal, which seemed to me a country teeming with riches and great natural resources. That I was a great friend to railroads, and that I was never in a country which I thought required railroads so much as the Transvaal. I expressed a hope, therefore, to see the day when the country would be penetrated by them in every direction—east, and south, and west. The President smiled at my strongly expressed aspiration, but did not give me any other reply.

Like every other town in the Transvaal, Pretoria shows signs of rapidly-growing prosperity. Public buildings and private dwelling-houses are springing up in every direction. The Post Office, recently finished, is capacious and commodious: and the new Government buildings for the accommodation of the Volksraad and the Courts of Justice, already commenced, but, as yet, only a few feet from the ground, and which cover a very large

space, promise to be very fine and imposing.
While at Pretoria I had ample opportunity
for observing many of the prevalent features
of both political and social life, and especially
of the condition of the large native population
of the town.

The Pretoria winter races took place during
my stay there. The races were very good
and well-conducted. There was a large and
orderly crowd who appeared thoroughly to
enjoy themselves, and their outing in that fine
and sunny climate. The Racecourse seemed a
good one, though rather hard owing to the
dry weather. It is in a very pretty spot
with picturesque surroundings.

The Kafirs, who are employed in great
numbers, and who are earning high wages
at their various occupations, are always to
be seen, either working hard, or, after the
hours of labour are over, amusing themselves

cheerfully, chatting at street corners, walking, gossiping, and talking, and gratifying themselves by giving vent to their very voluble tongues. Here also, as at Johannesburg, at Potchefstroom, and at Klerksdorp, I was forcibly struck with the large amount of English spoken, as well as of the number of English names over the various shops in the Transvaal towns. This is an interesting and important fact, which marks the tendency of the direction of future development. The country must certainly become more and more anglicised, in spite of the political efforts made to oppose it.

WATERBURG.

I LEFT Pretoria on July the 17th in a wagon with eight horses, accompanied by two friends, for an excursion into the Waterburg district of the Transvaal. On this occasion we travelled about one hundred and fifty miles north of Pretoria in the course of a fortnight, returning about the same distance back again. We had a half-breed servant named Sole with us, who made himself generally useful during our journey. All this time we camped out day and night, sleeping always in the open veldt, in true gipsy fashion.

We went by the Van der Vroom Poort,

having the Maalieburg range of mountains on
our left.

Our first night was spent at a farm called
" Polonia," belonging to a Russian Missionary
who has been for many years in the Transvaal.
He unites the pursuits of spiritual instruction
according to the tenets of the Greek Church,
with farming on a large scale. On leaving
" Polonia" we passed the large and picturesque
German Mission Station of " Hebron," which
is situated in the midst of a rich and fertile
valley. One night we outspanned at a spot
called the " Salt Pans." While breakfast was
being prepared the next morning, I walked
to see those wonderful " Salt Pans," which
were close to our camping ground. I descended by a steep path some six hundred or
seven hundred feet to the bottom. It is an
immense amphitheatre at the base of thickly
wooded hills. It is larger in extent than the

vast open excavation formed by the "Kimberley" Mine at Kimberley. The salt and soda brine is perpetually oosing from the bottom, and is continually being scraped up with a sort of wooden scraper into heaps, where, after a time, by the action of the atmosphere, it becomes crystallised. I picked up and brought away with me several crystals of pure salt. This is another of the marvels of the Transvaal, a country which abounds in natural wealth of all kinds, fitted for the service of man. These Salt Pans are the property of the Transvaal Government, which derives a considerable income from the tax imposed for taking away the salt, and soda, from them.

Frequently during our journey we outspanned just outside the Kafir kraals, and often entered into them ; one of my companions speaking the native, as well as the

Dutch languages very fluently. We were always received by both Boers, and Kafirs, very kindly. Sometimes we were accompanied by a large number of Kafirs for days. I remember once, counting as many as forty Kafirs sitting round our camp fire, clothed and unclothed, and in every variety of costume, from the old British Artillery tunic to the equally ancient pea coat, the bright-coloured blue morning jacket, and the cloak of Jackall skins. On this occasion they remained all night with us, keeping up the fire and indulging in endless and cheerful talk among themselves. When I wrapped myself in my kaross and turned into the wagon at night I left them talking. When I awoke in the early morning I found them talking still.

The country I saw in the Northern part of the Transvaal is very different, and far

more picturesque than it is in the South-West
or South-East, which have a close resemblance
to one another, in their bare, barren, treeless,
and dreary character. I saw some parts
which were really beautiful. One day we
drove for several miles through quite lovely
scenery. In passing along the road I was
forcibly reminded of the road between Braemar
and Mar Lodge, in Aberdeenshire, which it
strongly resembles. The road runs on the
side of the hill, sloping down to the rivulet
at the bottom, exactly like the river Dee,
and the Rooiburg, or red tinted, Mountain,
exactly resembles the heather on the Scottish
hills. It is altogether a charming spot, and
a perfect picture of fine scenery. There is a
large quantity of excellent and valuable timber
in this district, as well as abundant evidence
of mineral-bearing quartz. I believe that,
some day, other Johannesburgs are destined

to rise in the Northern part of the Transvaal, rivalling, or perhaps even eclipsing, the treasures already discovered in the Randt.

At the spot I have described, which is called Hartebeestepoort, not far from the banks of the Zand River, where there is a good quantity of excellent and valuable timber, there was quite a romantic scene one night. We were discussing, as usual, our evening meal round our camp fire. It was starlight, but otherwise we were in total darkness. In addition to ourselves, there were nine Kafirs, making a party of a dozen altogether. It was an intensely interesting and remarkable scene to me, to find myself surrounded by these wild fellows in perfectly friendly fashion, in the midst of the vast veldt, the silence and stillness only broken every now and then by the cry of the jackals howling in the distance.

On leaving here we travelled north towards Grouthock, which is situated in the midst of the Rhynoster range of mountains, being drawn by oxen, our horses following us, in order to give them rest, and so keep them fresher.

I was disappointed at the small quantity of game we found on our journey. We occasionally shot a springbok, and I thus had an opportunity of making myself acquainted with the delicious flavour of the South African venison. But the days of the enormous herds which once abounded in these regions are gone. They have been either exterminated by the Boers, or been driven far northward, into the interior of Africa, together with the lions and elephants, over whose former habitation I was travelling. There are still a good many koodoos, and hartebeestes in this neighbourhood, but I was not fortunate enough to come across them. Our commissariat was occasionally supplemented by a delicious bird, about the size of a pheasant, called the kooran, as well as by a few pheasants, partridges, and guinea fowls.

One afternoon we were exposed to a thrilling adventure, which, but for the merciful interposition of Providence, might have terminated in a most disastrous way. Suddenly, as we were driving along the road, through a dense wood, we discovered to the right of us the light of an immense bush fire. It was careering wildly along, fiercely burning, and sweeping everything before it. We saw it was coming swiftly towards the road we were travelling. We pulled up the horses, and taking out lucifer matches, jumped off the wagon, and tried to set alight to the grass, which was about five or six feet high, and very dry, close by us, in order to secure a

I

clear open space around us. But it was too late. The fierce fire, to the height of several feet, was rushing and crashing through the wood furiously towards us. Another moment, and we should have been within its terrible grasp, and wagon, horses. and ourselves infallibly burnt. It was in truth an awful crisis. We jumped back into the wagon and pushed frantically forward. Showers of sparks were already in the road. But, fortunately, the fire, which for a full half mile was burning behind us, was only a short distance in front of us, and, thank God, we happily escaped.

One of the great advantages I have derived from my tour is, that I have had many opportunities of communicating personally with so many men of different races, and all classes —British, Dutch, and natives.

During my present journey I had a most interesting conversation one morning with a transport driver, who was travelling by the northern part of the Transvaal, with three hundred lean cattle from the Cape Colony into Bechuanaland. He gave me some very valuable and important information with regard to Colonial feeling in the country districts of the Cape Colony. He was Colonial born, and a fine, handsome man of about forty—a descendant of the Scotch farmers, who emigrated to the Cape in 1820. His conversation impressed me much. He told me that the Colonists generally are loyal to the Queen to the backbone; but not to the British Government, which they consider has not represented their feelings and opinions, and has sacrificed their interests. They dislike the Colonial Government, and are not favourable to responsible Government, as they see it.

They would prefer being under the British Government direct, in spite of all its terrible mistakes and mishaps, from which they have so cruelly suffered. My informant's opinion was, that the present policy of the administration in Bechuanaland is not conducive to encourage emigration, as it puts artificial impediments in the way of farmers with small means settling there, which, he thought, they would do in crowds from the Colony, if they were allowed to do so on paying a quit rent, say of £10 or £15 per annum, instead of the high terms of £40 demanded at present. He had a very high opinion of Bechuanaland as a cattle-grazing country.

The Waterburg warm sulphur baths—to which I paid a visit, taking a hot bath myself, which was certainly much too hot for me, but which was otherwise refreshing, after nearly a fortnight's residence on the veldt, where there is a decided scarcity of water, both for drinking and washing purposes—are situated about seventy miles north of Pretoria. They

are extensively patronised by the Boers, and
are said to be most efficacious in every variety
of rheumatic and gouty complaints. They are
strongly impregnated with sulphur, and might
be made very attractive in the hands of anyone
of enterprise, who would construct a suitable
establishment of baths, fit for patients who
would be quite ready to pay handsomely for
them, instead of the miserably primitive and
wretched receptacles, called baths, into which
the highly excellent natural sulphur water is
conveyed, and used by the motley crowd of
invalids I saw there.

From the Waterburg warm baths our route
lay to the southward, across the Springbok
Flats, to the Nylstroom road, along which, in
two days more, we accomplished the intervening
distance of about seventy miles back to
Pretoria, thus concluding a most interesting
and instructive journey into the northern part

of the Transvaal. During all this time, with the exception of the first night, I lived entirely in our wagon, sleeping in it every night, and having every meal (which consisted principally of the game we shot on the way), cooked at the various camp fires kindled on the veldt, and drinking nothing but tea. I saw much, of course, of the Kafirs in their kraals, as well as of the Boers in their tents and wagons, in my trek through this wilderness.

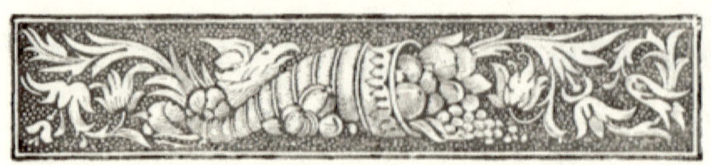

PRETORIA TO NATAL.

AFTER reaching Pretoria, I stayed only two days there, engaged in bidding farewell to my numerous friends, and making preparations for my next long journey into Natal. I left Pretoria for Johannesburg by coach, on the 1st of August, and started from the latter town at five o'clock in the morning of the 3rd, in very cold weather and pitch dark, by the post cart. This most uncomfortable vehicle is a kind of wagonette, with somewhat dilapidated canvas curtains, through which the wind whistled most unpleasantly, being utterly insufficient to keep out the cold. It is drawn by eight horses, and has cramped seats for eight or ten passengers. On this occasion there were seven others besides myself. In addition the mail bags, were crammed inconveniently under the seats. In this post cart I travelled for three days and two nights by way of Richmond, Heidelburg, Standerton,—where cattle rearing and horse breeding is successfully carried on,—and Newcastle, which will be remembered as having been the base of operations during the Boer war, and also as the place where the final treaty of Peace was drawn up and signed by the joint Commission, to Eland's Laagte, the present terminus of the Natal railway, thirteen miles beyond Lady-smith. At Eland's Laagte a very promising coal field is being worked, from which great and important results are expected in the future. Soon after crossing the Transvaal border we passed the battle fields of Laing's

CEMETERY, MAJUBA HILL.

Nek, Majuba Hill, and Ingogo, names indelibly
associated with one of the saddest, as well as
most humiliating, episodes of English modern
military history, in connection with the Transvaal War of 1881. I gazed mournfully on
Majuba Hill, that black spot of bitter memories
to every Briton, and of natural exultation
and pride to the Boers ; and on Colley's
grave, the unfortunate commander, whose
unhappy and most unaccountable military
blunder led to the lamentable and fatal defeat,
which cost him his life, and resulted in the
miserable fiasco—the retrocession of the Transvaal to the Boers. It is impossible to estimate
the damage done to British influence, prestige,
and power by the political consequences resulting
from that disastrous day.

The south-eastern part of the Transvaal is
as bare, and treeless, and altogether as
uninteresting and unattractive as the south

K

western region, between Bechuanaland and Klerksdorp, through which I had travelled a few weeks previously. The instant, however, the border is crossed, and Natal is entered, the scene is at once changed, and the beauty of the surrounding country becomes apparent. Instead of the flat, wearisome desert of the Transvaal, undulating hills, clothed with verdure, and an extensive panorama of broad and fertile plains meets the eye.

GOVERNMENT HOUSE, MARITZBURG.

MARITZBURG.

AFTER leaving Ladysmith, I proceeded to Maritzburg, the seat of Government of Natal. This picturesque town is in a charming situation, the surrounding scenery being extremely pretty. The town itself, is well laid out, the streets being wide, and in most cases edged with trees. Amongst its public buildings may be mentioned the new House of Assembly, of which Sir John Akerman is Speaker. It is a handsome edifice, well arranged, and economically constructed at a cost of £20,000. A life-size statue of Her Majesty is to be erected in the front of the building, the pedestal of which is already *in situ.*

While staying at Government House, and enjoying the kind hospitality of Sir Charles and Lady Mitchell, my ear was often gladdened by the sound of the cavalry bugle and the roll of the drum, those striking symbols of British sway, as the troops passed my window in their early morning rides. I am persuaded that these outward evidences of latent power, impress not only the minds of Englishmen, but of natives also, in this distant land. There cannot be a doubt of the influence exercised by the British race over the aboriginal inhabitants of South Africa. That this should be used, at all times, with justice, tact, and discretion, "goes without saying;" but that it is a factor of great effect on their minds is unquestionable.

DURBAN.

THE railway journey from Maritzburg to Durban, a distance of fifty-seven miles by road, is long and rather tedious travelling on account of the slow pace. The line (a single one), which seems to have been very skilfully engineered, is necessarily constructed with such steep gradients that this seems inevitable. The long stoppages at stations might be certainly improved. Durban is the prettiest as well as one of the cleanest, and most well-ordered towns I have seen in South Africa. I was at once struck with the Town Hall, a magnificent building, recently

erected, and generally stated to be, although
not the largest, in some respects the hand-
somest in South Africa. The total cost of
construction was about £50,000, and it is
worthy of note that in their selection of an
architect, the Corporation of Durban did not
have to go beyond their own town, an
efficient man being found in Mr. P. M.
Dudgeon. The building is of the Corinthian
order of architecture, having a frontage of
206 feet, with a depth of 270 feet. It is
prettily situated, and is a striking proof of
what colonists can do when an occasion
demanding skill, and perseverance, arises. There
are several other fine buildings in the town.
A stranger coming from the Transvaal is
immediately impressed with the contrast
between the careless indifference, which marks
the absence of proper municipal arrangements
in the towns of the South African Republic,

TOWN HALL, DURBAN.

and the proofs of their presence in an energetic British community. The Natalians certainly deserve the greatest credit for the way in which they carry on the business and manage the public affairs of their prosperous, and thriving town, which has a population of 17,000, of whom about 9,000 are Europeans. Recent commercial returns show that the trade of Natal, of which Durban, as the seaport town, is the centre, is rapidly increasing.

The imports during the first three-quarters of the year 1888 were about two millions; and in 1889, during the same period, they had risen to three millions. The exports during 1888 were one million; for the same period in 1889 they were one million and a quarter. Imports have advanced 50 per cent., exports by 25 per cent. Customs revenue has advanced by 25 per cent., and if the receipts be maintained, which is more than probable, the total income for the year from this source will reach £350,000. It is anticipated that the combined trade of Natal for the year 1889 will not be far short of six millions sterling. The increase is a substantial one, and, what is more satisfactory, is that there appears to be every reasonable prospect that the trade will go on increasing by leaps and bounds. Affairs are in a generally prosperous state, and a good sign is to be found in the fact that the emigration returns are also rapidly rising.

The gigantic Harbour Works, commenced and now nearly successfully completed for the purpose of removing the bar, according to the plans both of Sir John Coode, and subsequently of his pupil, their late lamented engineer, Mr. Innes, and under the active personal superintendence of their distinguished townsman

HARBOUR WORKS, DURBAN.

the Chairman of the Harbour Board, comprise an undertaking of which the citizens of Durban may well be proud. Nor is less credit due to them, and to their spirited leaders, for their enterprise in so rapidly pushing on their railway to the Transvaal border, in the confident expectation that they will be the first to bring the benefits of that most necessary modern mode of conveyance, both for passengers and goods, into the heart of the Transvaal Republic.

The Harbour Works, the Railway, and the Durban Town Hall are all works of sufficient magnitude to give undoubted evidence of the public spirit and unconquerable energy of the people of Natal.

The inhabitants of Durban are fortunate in possessing picturesque surroundings to their pretty town. The "Berea," one of its most attractive spots, is an elevated suburb where

L

many of the principal merchants, and others have their residences. It commands a lovely prospect over the bay, and a beautiful view of the country inland.

During my stay at Durban I paid visits to two of the most remarkable places in the neighbourhood. These were the Natal Central Sugar Company's manufactory at Mount Edgcumbe, and the famous Trappist establishment at Marionhill. The sugar manufactory is situated on a farm of some 8,000 acres, about 15 miles from Durban. A short railway ride brought me to it. I was courteously received by the manager, Monsieur Dumat. This gentleman, a Frenchman of great experience in the manufacture of sugar both in India and Mauritius, has been at Mount Edgcumbe for the last ten years. He is remarkable for the way in which he maintains order and control over all his numerous native workmen. In

the mill itself there are 160 men employed,
everyone of whom is a Coolie. There is not
a single white man on the premises, excepting
two English clerks in the counting house. I
was astonished at the perfect order which
reigned in the mill, where I spent some time.
Everyone appeared to perform his allotted task
with activity, cheerfulness, and untiring perseverance. Monsieur Dumat told me he could
never get the same steady work from white
workmen. He seems to govern them all with
perfect tact and kindness. Some of them have
been with him for many years. There are
about 900 other men, Kafirs and Coolies,
employed on the farm. I was shown all the
various processes of sugar manufacture, from
the crushing of the cane, to the crystallising of
the sugar. The first sorts are ready for sale
in forty-eight hours; other qualities require a
week, and again even as much as six months

to perfect them. There is some wonderful machinery in the mill.

The Trappist establishment at Marionhill is one which should be seen by everyone visiting Natal. It is reached by rail from Durban in about an hour's ride to the Pine Town station. A drive from thence of about four miles brings a visitor to Marionhill. The monks, as is well known, are under a vow of strict silence. I was met by one of them at the station, who drove me in a waggonette to the Trappist farm. Here I was met by, and presented to, the Abbot. He is the real leader and director of this re-markable establishment. He devoted three hours to taking me over it, and showing me all the various industries and works which are carried on. About two hundred brothers are there at present, but more are expected shortly. and upwards of one hundred sisters, and about three hundred Kafirs. The latter are taught,

not only the ordinary branches of a practical
education (of course including religion), but all
sorts of handicraft. It is, emphatically, a school
of technical education. Everything is manu-
factured and made at Marionhill, from the substantial bullock wagons, and the delicate
spiders, to the baking of bread, the building of
houses, stables, and cattle kairs, the printing
of periodicals, and book-binding. Work is the
great and leading feature of the Trappist creed.
The motive power is religion. Its controlling
influence is here complete.

I came away quite amazed at all I saw, as
well as pleased at the attention I received
from the Abbot. He is certainly a very remarkable man, of great natural gifts, and
indomitable energy and power. He is sixty-
five years of age. He was born on the shores
of Lake Constance; and before he took to
studying for the Roman Catholic Church in a

German University, he was employed, as he
told me, in early life in the care of cattle at
his native home.

The Trappist farm is beautifully situated,
and within its area contains some really fine
scenery. The Kafir women's part of the establishment is distinct, and quite half a mile
distant from the men's quarters. Women are
taught to sew, and sing, to cut out and make
dresses, to cook, clean, and go through all the
usual routine of household work. The costume
of the female Trappists, who, as well as the
male, are highly educated, is scarlet serge, with
white aprons. The men are clothed in brown
serge.

I was struck with the admirable arrangement
of the stables, constructed for twenty horses,
and of the cow and cattle sheds. All the
engineering works also show evidences of the
complete knowledge of science possessed by the

" brothers," and their energetic leader. I came away much interested, and wonderfully impressed with all I had seen in this remarkable institution.

Up to the present time the defences of the Colony have been in a very backward state but I was glad to find that a battery is in course of construction, commanding the entrance to the Bay, which is to be armed with guns of the latest pattern, one of them having recently arrived at Durban.

Having passed ten very pleasant days at Durban and its neighbourhood, I embarked, on the 15th of August, on board the coasting steamer, *Anglian*, for Port Elizabeth. I had a terrible experience of the annoyance of the present mode of embarking passengers at Durban. After attempting to get over the Bar in a tremendous sea, we were obliged to put back into the Harbour thoroughly drenched. Once more

attempting it, we succeeded after another good
wetting in getting alongside the *Anglian*, where
we remained at anchor until the morning.
waiting for the Cargo Boat we were obliged
to leave behind, rolling and pitching all night.
The eastern coast of South Africa is subject
to weather which is often very rough and
stormy; and I was, unluckily, destined to
experience it. I certainly had a most dis-
agreeable time in making this short voyage.
After touching at East London, where extensive harbour works are being constructed,
I was landed at Port Elizabeth (after three
days' knocking about at sea) on the 18th.
being let down, like St. Paul, in a basket,
from the deck of the *Anglian* to the tug,
which took me to the pier in the open
roadstead. Right glad was I to get on *terra
firma* again.

PORT ELIZABETH.

Port Elizabeth (Algoa Bay) which is generally known as the "Liverpool" of South Africa, is the chief seaport of the Eastern Province, its trade being steadily increased by the development of the Transvaal Gold Fields, and the growth of the interior towns of the Cape Colony. It is a thriving business town. Its inhabitants, like those of Natal, are thoroughly energetic and active in the pursuit of their various mercantile avocations, and number about 12,000, a large proportion being Europeans.

The town contains many fine buildings, the

most conspicuous being the Town Hall and
Public Library combined, which is a striking
edifice, erected at a cost of £26,000. Attached to it is the market, leading out of
which is a splendid and capacious hall,
180 feet long by 90 feet broad. Here I
saw a curious and unique scene. Long tables
were extended along its entire length, on
which were arranged large heaps of ostrich
feathers, carefully tied up, and sampled for
sale. Port Elizabeth is the staple market
for this industry. The value of the feathers
I saw, I was told, was something fabulous.

Port Elizabeth is a handsome town. In
the upper part of it, called the Hill, there
are many good private residences, and an
excellent club house, at which I stayed, and
enjoyed the kind hospitality, courteously extended to me.

A large, well kept, and conveniently laid

out botanical garden, which is much resorted to, is a great attraction to the town. There is also an excellent hospital at Port Elizabeth. I was much pleased with its appearance, and with the arrangements made for the comfort of the patients. The ventilation struck me as being particularly perfect. There is accommodation for 100 patients, male and female. A well-arranged children's ward, attracts much attention, especially with the lady visitors.

There is, in addition, a good water supply obtained from Van Staden's River, distant about twenty-seven miles from the town, at a cost of about £150,000.

There are several Churches, including Trinity Church, St. Augustine's Roman Catholic Cathedral, the Scottish Presbyterian Church, and a Congregational Church, upon which no less a sum than £7,715 was expended.

Previously to leaving Port Elizabeth, the

following address was presented to me by
the Fellows of the Royal Colonial Institute
resident there :—

To Sir Frederick Young, K.C.M.G.,
A Vice-President of the Royal Colonial Institute.

" Sir,

" We, the undersigned Fellows of the
Royal Colonial Institute, take advantage of
your presence amongst us to join in the expression of hearty welcome to South Africa,
which has greeted you in the several towns
where you have met the Members of the
Institute, with which you have been so long
and honourably connected.

" We are mindful of the valuable services
which you have so long rendered to our
Institute, as Honorary Secretary, the indefa-
tigable zeal ever displayed by you in for-
warding the interests of the Colonies of Great
Britain ; and that the success of the Institution,

over which you now preside, as one of the Vice-Presidents, is in no small degree due to your exertions. We venture to hope that your visit to South Africa has been an agreeable one, and that with renewed health you will return home to resume and continue the valuable services you have heretofore rendered, and that the Royal Colonial Institute may continue to flourish under the auspices of the distinguished men who so ably guard its interests."

GRAHAMSTOWN.

WHILE I was at Port Elizabeth I paid a flying visit to Grahamstown. A railway journey of rather over one hundred miles carried me there. The railway runs through the veldt, where wild elephants are still strictly preserved. There are said to be more than one hundred of these animals in the district. They occasionally do great damage to the line. During my stay I was hospitably entertained by the Bishop. I had already heard that Grahamstown was noted for its natural charms, and its appearance certainly did not disappoint me. Beautiful in situation, it merits the high praises which have been bestowed upon it. It has also acquired a reputation for being the seat of learning, and the centre of the principal educational establishments of the Colony. The Bishop having kindly provided me with a carriage, I drove to see the various objects of interest in the neighbourhood. I first went to the Botanical Gardens, which are very striking. They contain a large collection of rare and valuable specimens of both arboriculture and horticulture. They are admirably kept, and are very ornamental. I next drove round the Mountain road. This is a beautiful drive of seven miles back into the town. The views of the surrounding country are superb. It is a priceless boon to the inhabitants of Grahamstown to possess such an attractive and health-giving spot, for their recreation and enjoyment. I afterwards visited the Museum, where there is a most interesting and valuable collection of animal, vegetable, and mineral curiosities, both ancient and modern. I also went over the Prison, and recorded in the visitors' book my favourable opinion of the arrangements made for the health and comfort of the prisoners. They appeared to me to be all that could reasonably be expected, or desired. I also went to see the Kafir school, carried on under the careful management of the Rev. Mr. and Mrs. M——.

I regretted that time did not permit of my visiting the celebrated Ostrich Farm of Mr. Arthur Douglass, at Heatherton Towers, about fifteen miles from Grahamstown. Mr. Douglass has the largest and most successful Ostrich Farm in the Colony, in addition to which he is the patentee of an egg hatching machine, or incubator, which is very much used in various parts of South Africa. The export of feathers has increased rapidly, and has become one of the chief exports of the Colony, as whilst in 1868 the quantity exported was valued at £70,000, in 1887 it had reached the value of £365,587. This is by no means the largest amount appearing under the head of exports during recent years, as in 1882 the value of feathers exported was £1,093,989. It is estimated that during the past half-century the total weight of the feathers exported has been more than one thousand tons. The Cape Colony has, in fact, had a monopoly of the ostrich industry, but in 1884 several shipments of ostriches took place to South Australia, the Argentine Republic, and to California, and the Government of the Cape Colony, being alarmed, that the Colony was in danger of losing its lucrative monopoly, imposed an export tax of £100 on each ostrich, and £5 on each ostrich egg exported.

X

PORT ELIZABETH TO CAPE TOWN.

On my return to Port Elizabeth, I spent another day or two there, and left on the evening of Monday, the 26th of August, by railway for Cape Town. This long journey of between eight hundred and nine hundred miles occupies nearly two days and two nights. It was the last I took in South Africa. The country, generally speaking, is very much of the same kind as that northward, over the Karoo, and in the southern part of the Transvaal. High land,—in the neighbourhood of Nieupoort 5,050 feet above the sea level,—flat, bare, and treeless. It is certainly a very desolate-looking country to

HEX RIVER PASS.

travel over in winter. Nearing Cape Town, however, I ought not to omit to mention the Hex River Pass. The scenery here is certainly very grand, and is some of the best of its kind I have seen in South Africa. The railway, which winds through it by a succession of zigzags from a great height, is another of the many triumphs of engineering skill which are to be found in all parts of the world. The fine views of the Pass, when I traversed it, were heightened by the tops of the mountains being tinged with a wreath of snow. From Hex River the route to Cape Town lay through a rich and fertile valley, conveying ample proofs of the agricultural value and resources of this part of the Cape Colony. I arrived at Cape Town in the afternoon of the following Wednesday. Here I spent another pleasant week, seeing various friends.

One of the last duties which devolved upon

me before leaving South Africa—at the urgent invitation of some of my friends—was to deliver an address at Cape Town on Imperial Federation. This I did at the hall of the Young Men's Christian Society, to a large and attentive audience.*

On the 4th of September I left Cape Town in the s.s. *Athenian;* and, after a pleasant and rapid voyage of eighteen days, touching only at Madeira on the way, I landed safely at Southampton on Sunday the 22nd.

I have now given an account of the prominent features of my tour, during which, in the course of five months, I travelled about twelve thousand miles by sea, and four thousand by land.

I proceed to touch as briefly as I can, on a few of the public questions, and other matters of interest which have arrested my attention while I was in South Africa.

---

* See Appendix.

CLIMATE.

THE climate of South Africa has already been so well, and exhaustively described, in the admirable and interesting paper, read at a meeting of the Royal Colonial Institute, on the 13th November, 1888, by Dr. Symes Thompson, that it seems superfluous for anyone to attempt to add anything to what such an eminent professional authority has said on the subject. But I cannot help remarking that, from my own personal experience, I can fully corroborate all he has said in its favour. The winter climate seems perfect. The atmosphere is so bright and clear, the air is so dry, and the

sun is so agreeably warm in the day, although
it is cold and frosty at night, that I think
it must be as salubrious, as it has been to
me most enjoyable. I found this the case
everywhere, especially in the higher altitudes,
and on the elevated veldt of the Transvaal.
For myself, I never had an hour's illness
during the whole winter I passed in South
Africa; and this I attribute entirely to the
purity of the air, and the dryness of the
climate. One thing it is necessary to be
cautious about, and I have an impression that
it is not sufficiently attended to, and is consequently frequently the cause of illness, and
injury. There is always a sudden great
variation of the temperature immediately the
sun goes down. To a sensitive person this is
instantly perceptible. In the afternoon everyone ought to be very careful in guarding
against this change; and should be provided

with an extra garment to put on at sunset, in order to avoid a dangerous chill. I strongly advise, also, temperance in the use of alcoholic beverages, which, in my opinion, are far too freely consumed. I have noticed too much drinking among all classes. This cannot be necessary, or very conducive to the preservation of health, and the prolongation of life, in a climate like that of South Africa.

It is to be earnestly hoped, that a good. and thoroughly efficient system of sanitary organisation may be speedily established in all the rapidly-growing towns throughout the country, especially in the Transvaal. Terrible neglect in this respect has been the cause of exceptional sickness, and great mortality in the past, for which the climate is not responsible. In order, too, to render the undoubted excellencies of the South African climate more attractive to invalids, who ought more largely to avail themselves of its advantages, it would be an excellent thing, as well as undoubtedly a paying speculation, if better hotels, fitted up in all respects with all modern European improvements, were established both at Cape Town, and at all the other principal towns up country, as well.

THE NATIVE QUESTION.

THE native question is one of the most prominent and difficult ones to deal with in South Africa. The great preponderance of the native over the white races, and the different theories of treating them prevalent between the English and Dutch, render it one of the most perplexing problems to solve. The wisest and most experienced people, with whom I have communicated on the subject are of opinion that the natives are so far behind us in civilisation that they must be regarded as mere children. This means, however, that they are not to be treated harshly, but, on the

o

contrary, with the utmost fairness and justice, and that they must be under the guidance of a controlling and firmly governing hand. They respect authority, when they have confidence in its being exercised with impartiality. They have a great deal of natural shrewdness, and they must never be deceived. Alas! I heard of frequent instances of this having been done, in times past, by those who have represented the British Government. Promises have been made to them which have been carelessly broken, and this means ruin to the prestige in their minds of the British name.

From the wonderful and ever-increasing development which has taken place in the northern part of South Africa since the dis-covery of diamonds and gold, causing the employment of thousands upon thousands of native Kafirs at high wages, their social position is being materially changed. They are really becoming "masters of the situation." Their constant contact with white people is having the effect of introducing among them the germs of an incipient civilisation. The mode of treating them by the British and the Dutch is, undoubtedly, very different. A far harsher and more cruel method has been in vogue by the Dutch towards them, than would be tolerated by the British. But, from the cause to which I have alluded, the day has arrived when all this old system is sensibly changing; and the Draconian code of the Boers, from the force of circumstances, is becoming modified every day. I have made it my business to observe carefully all the signs of the times, on this native question during my tour. I have seen the Kafirs in thousands working in the mines at Kimberley, and Klerksdorp, and Johannesburg; I have observed them in multitudes employed in extensive building

operations at Pretoria, and as labourers on the
public works at Maritzburg and Durban, and
at the other great shipping centres of Port
Elizabeth and Cape Town ; I have noticed
them in their capacity of servants in private
houses, and I frankly confess that no evidence
has been brought before me to indicate, that
they are harshly or unkindly treated. On the
contrary, it appeared to me that they are
receiving good wages, and are everywhere well
cared for and comfortable. They are naturally
a lively and a happy race, and I have seen
them as cheerful and light-hearted in the
town, as in their kraals on the wild and open
veldt.

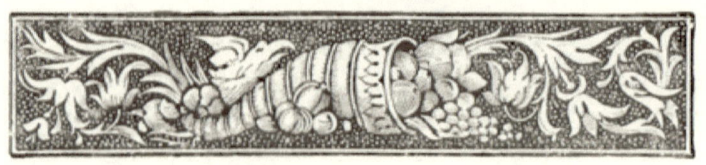

RAILWAYS.

I HAVE already mentioned that, in my interview with the President, Paul Kruger, I told him that I was never in a country, which, in my opinion, required railways more than the Transvaal, and that I hoped to see the day when it would be penetrated by them in every direction. It is much to be regretted that there is so much jealous rivalry, inducing fierce contention, as to the precise direction, from the east, or south, or west, railroads should enter the Transvaal. I contend, that there is such a prospect of future enormous development in this wonderful centre of South Africa, that there is no need for all this rivalry, but that there is room for many lines in which all may participate and prosper, in the future.   Political considerations have undoubtedly complicated a question, which I should wish to regard solely from its commercial aspect.

Personally, I am anxious to see the line over the ground which I have myself treked, pushed on as speedily as possible, from Kimberley to Vryburg, and thence through British Bechuanaland to Mafeking, and so on, northwards, into the Matabele country, with branches eastward into the Transvaal.   But I should like, also, to see the contemplated line constructed from Kimberley, through the Orange Free State, to Bloemfontein; and the Delagoa Bay Railway carried on to Pretoria, as well as the Natal line to Johannesburg; and, in fact, any other, whether through Swaziland, or elsewhere, which commercial enterprise may hereafter project.   They will all have the effect of opening up the Transvaal—the El Dorado of

South Africa—and meeting the demand for the transit of the enormous traffic, with which the old system of bullock wagons is utterly unable to grapple, and which, consequently, is so fearfully congested. The transport riders will have ample compensation, under the new system, in their increased employment in the conveyance of goods from the various stations to their actual destination. It was in this way the coach proprietors, without loss, and with great advantage to themselves, became the great and successful railway carriers, when stage coaches were superseded by railways in England.

Since I arrived in England, Sir Gordon Sprigg, in an important speech delivered at Kimberley, referred to the question of railway extension from that town in the following words:—" With the South Atlantic Ocean for our base, we started with our railway, and then we came up to Kimberley.

From this place we have only fifty or
sixty miles to go over, and then we come
to the border of this province, and of British
Bechuanaland. Farther north, we get to that
ill-defined sphere, called the sphere of influence,
that extended the power of Britain in South
Africa, as far as the Zambesi. . . . Now
that we have our railway up to Kimberley, we
have the British South African Company to
take it in hand, and the object of the Government is to see that we have an extension line
into these territories which will, in time to
come, be recognised as portions of the Cape
Colony. Gentlemen, I and my colleagues have
come to the conclusion that we cannot better
advance the best interests of South Africa
than by joining hand-in-hand to advance
British interests westward of the Transvaal
State, and right up to the Zambesi. Well,
then, that being so, I may say, that the first

object of the Company, in order to carry on
their operations to the best purpose, is to construct a railway from Kimberley to Vryburg.
The section from Kimberley to Warrenton has,
of course, first to be undertaken, and from
there on to Vryburg, as the second section.
The Company are in possession of the requisite
funds to carry out this great work; and there
is no reason why it should not be accomplished
before many months are over. The Government of this country (Cape Colony) have come
to the conclusion that it is desirable that this
work should be carried out, and an arrangement has been made between the Government
of this country and Mr. Rhodes as representing
the British South African Company, whereby
a railway starting from Kimberley up to
Vryburg will be constructed by the British
South African Company. Certain conditions
have been entered into between the Company

and the Government of this Colony, under which the Government of the Colony will have the right to take over the railway at any time they think proper, on certain conditions to be entered into by one side or the other. This railway extension is to be immediately proceeded with. You may take it as a moral certainty that you will be able to travel by railway up to Warrenton, some time in the course of next year. The Government have come to the conclusion that it is in the interests of South Africa that this work shall be carried on ; that, in short, it would be highly in-judicious to place any obstacles in the way of an undertaking which is calculated to have so beneficial an effect on the prospects of this part of Her Majesty's Empire." This Speech, coming from the Premier of the Cape Colony, requires no comment from me, beyond the expression of my satisfaction at its having been made.

COLONISATION.

COLONISATION is a subject on which I wish to say a few words. The definition given by Adam Smith of the three elements of national wealth, "Land, Labour, and Capital," cannot be too often repeated. How to blend them in proper proportions, is a problem, which has puzzled generations of statesmen, philosophers, and philanthropists. I have always been a warm advocate for colonisation. It appears to me to be a question of such supreme national importance, that I think it ought to be undertaken by the State. This, of course, means, that it is possible, as it is undoubtedly indispensable, to get a Government to act wisely and well. In order to have a chance of its being successful, colonisation must be conducted on sound principles and practice.

In South Africa I have seen millions of acres of fertile land—in Bechuanaland, in Natal, in the Eastern and Western provinces of the Cape Colony, to say nothing of the Transvaal—capable of supporting many thousands of our surplus population. But I have also satisfied myself, that it is no use whatever to transplant those, who are unfitted for it. Instead of a success, certain failure will be the result of an attempt so unwise. Colonial life is alone suitable for the enterprising, energetic, steady, and industrious men, and women, who are determined, with patience and courage, to overcome the difficulties and trials, which they must certainly encounter on the road to ultimate success. South Africa is a land of promise for them. It is by no means so for the feeble, the self-indulgent, the helplessly dependent class, of whom, unfortunately, we have so large a number in the over-populated Old Country. Cordial co-operation with the self-governing colonies is also absolutely indispensable to ensure success in any national system of colonisation. It is equally essential that a strict selection of the right sort of people should be made. According, too, to their positions in life, they must be provided with sufficient means to support them on their first arrival, while they are settling themselves, and their crops are growing, and they are acquiring knowledge, of the natural conditions of the new land, to which they have been transplanted.

These are the principles necessary to be observed in any national system of colonisation. They apply to all the other British Colonies, equally with South Africa, in order to prevent failure, and command success.

While speaking of this subject, I should like to mention a suggestion for a system of special colonisation, which may well attract the serious attention of the Home Government, with the view of encouraging and promoting it.

In the military garrisons, comprising the British troops, quartered in South Africa, there are a considerable number of steady, and well-conducted married men. non-commissioned officers and soldiers, who, having been stationed for some time in the midst of its genial climate, and pleasant surroundings, would, I feel satisfied, like, if sufficient inducement were offered them, to make South Africa their permanent home. If, therefore, a military colony were established at the expense of the Home Government in a well and wisely-selected spot and under proper and judicious arrangement, it would probably be, not only a great boon to a number of deserving British subjects, but would be attended with success, and be a politic, and interesting factor in the art of colonisation.

I earnestly commend the idea to those, who would have to deal with it, as an experiment, eminently worthy of their attention and support.

THE POLITICAL SITUATION.

THE political situation of South Africa is the last subject to which I shall refer. I am quite aware that this is a very difficult and delicate question to touch upon, but it would be impossible for anyone like myself, to whom it has presented itself so prominently during my tour, to avoid some allusion to it. I shall endeavour to state my impressions impartially and fairly.

Before I went to South Africa I had formed a general opinion on this vitally important and very critical subject. My previous views have been most thoroughly confirmed, and painfully accentuated by all I have seen, and heard, and gathered, on the spot. The mournful mismanagement of South African affairs during the last twenty-five years, and most especially during the last decade, has been truly lamentable, and cannot fail to awaken the saddest feelings on the part of every loyal Briton, and true-hearted patriot.

The absence of continuous, wise, and statesmanlike policy, which has for the most part marked the tone of those, who have had the Imperial guidance and control of South African affairs in the past, has had the effect of sowing the seeds of enmity to the Government of the Mother Country, which it will require all the wisdom, and tact, and conciliatory sympathy possible to be displayed in the future, in dealing with this magnificent part of the Empire, to allay. It will demand the greatest skill to prevent the permanent alienation, and

Q

estrangement of South Africa from Great Britain.

This has all been brought about by our unaccountably careless and culpable want of accurate knowledge at home, of the actual situation. We lost a splendid chance of consolidating South Africa in a homogeneous union under the British crown. Our insular in difference, our ignorance, the fierce animosity of our party political prejudices, made us neglect the opportunity. It has had the effect of creating the sorest feelings against us, on the part of the large English population, spread over the land, which is uncontaminated and uninfluenced by the party spirit of local colonial politicians. It is melancholy, and most deplorable to observe the indications of this feeling, which are constantly apparent. The old love for the British flag is still widely cherished : but it was impossible for me to shut my eyes to the evidence so continually brought before me, that the British Government is neither loved nor respected. No confidence whatever is felt in it—and no wonder! Everywhere there are proofs of how all have been allowed to suffer and smart under it.

Either from ignorance, or carelessness, or indifference—probably from all combined—and perhaps even unconsciously, but at the same time as surely, we have deceived the Natives, the Boers, and the Colonists. This is only the natural consequence of the feeble, vacillating, uncertain course, which is followed, when the State machine is guided without compass, and where there is no firmness, nor courage at the national helm. What we have to do, however, now, is to advocate union and co-operation between the two dominant races—the British and the Dutch—and to do all we can to promote harmony and goodwill between them. True, their mental character, and natural instincts are different. Our own race is essentially energetic and progressive; while theirs is slow, unemotional, and phlegmatic. But if sympathy, and tact, and cordial good temper, are invariably practised in our intercourse with them, I am persuaded it will ultimately have the effect of promoting co-operation in securing their mutual interests. This, I trust, will ultimately neutralise the effect of the fatal course of past political action, which unnecessarily developed race jealousies, and stimulated national friction and animosity; and will bring about in the future, a blending of the Dutch in friendly union and fellowship with the British, such as has been undreamed of in the past.

Among many expressions of opinion on the subject of the political situation made to me while I was in South Africa, I received the following communication from a gentleman of

prominent position in one of the principal towns
of the Cape Colony. It appears to me of such
importance that I avail myself of this opportunity of giving publicity to it.

"The fact of your arrival at very short
notice, combined with the fact that there are
only a few Fellows of the Royal Colonial
Institute resident here, will probably prevent the
presentation of any formal address of welcome
to you.

"Nevertheless, to a section of the community
which is animated by patriotic jealousy for the
rights and dignity of the Crown throughout
South Africa, your visit is regarded with
feelings of genuine satisfaction, and our hopes
are encouraged, that your visit may result in
some good to the cause, which we have at
heart.

"You are doubtless acquainted well enough
with the principal events of great national

moment of recent years in South Africa.
From whatever point of view politicians may
like to regard the end of the Transvaal war,
any resident in this country can be only too
well aware of the fact that one result of that
terrible experience has been, a material weaken-
ing of respect for English people, and for the
rights of the Crown throughout the Cape Colony.

"Since the period referred to, a very powerful
Dutch-Africander combination has come into
existence, and there can be no doubt but that
one object of such a body, is the severance of
all but nominal ties between the Cape, and
Great Britain.

"However visionary such hopes as these must
for a long series of years remain, the fact of
their existence, and of their being in a variety
of ways advanced from time to time, has a
very marked influence upon all classes of people
in this country.

"For instance, the youth of the country are influenced to hope for a time, when they shall be members of an independent State; and while on the one hand they may not see any immediate prospect of a change in such a direction being effected, nevertheless they lessen their interest in, and their respect for, the Crown of England and its attributes, and thus grow up comparatively devoid of any sound patriotism, even to their native country: and, above all, without any touch of that enthusiasm, which is ever engendered by high national traditions.

"That some momentous changes are likely to occur in South Africa, and that possibly, before very long, all are agreed. The question only remains in what direction will these changes tend?—towards some Foreign Continental Power, towards a Confederation with the existing Dutch Republics, or in the direction of a strengthening of the union with England ?

"It is sometimes surmised, and this not merely by extreme men, but by quiet and experienced observers of events in this country, that the large population, mainly British, which has been attracted to the Gold Fields of the Transvaal, is unlikely to endure much longer the systematic misgovernment and suppression, to which they are subjected by men of avowedly anti-English sympathies, and pledged to a policy directed to check British progress by all means.

"What form the suggested revolt in the Transvaal may take is not likely to be revealed, until some overt step towards its execution has been taken. We would all desire that the end in view should be secured by peaceful means, and that the Transvaal should become a part and parcel of British territory.

" To effect a revival of loyalty to England
in the Cape Colony, and to influence the
destinies of other States in the direction of
union with England, should surely be the hope
and endeavour of all true Englishmen, whether
in this Colony, or elsewhere.

" And the end in view is not an easy one
to attain in a country, where the majority of
Europeans consider that they, or their com-
patriots, inflicted disgrace, and a permanent
loss of influence upon the Imperial Troops on
the one hand, and the Imperial British Government on the other.

" The application of any remedy seems to
lie more with the Sovereign personally, or Her
Majesty's immediate advisers in England, than
with any Governor, and High Commissioner, or
Cabinet of Cape Ministers.

" For *quâ* Governor, the Queen's Representative at the Cape, is necessarily checked, or

R

controlled by the Ministry of the day, his
Constitutional advisers, and the presence in
the Cape Parliament of a dominant force of
the essentially non-English, or Africander party,
must necessarily also have a very material
influence upon Ministers, who depend upon a
majority of votes for the retention of their
office.

"In short, the problem in the Cape Colony
is one, which happily does not exist in either
of the other great dependencies of the Crown;
it is altogether peculiar to South Africa, of
which, after all, England acquired possession
by conquest, and, having acquired it, has never
completely won the adhesion of the Dutch
inhabitants, who resent such acts of Government as the abolition of slavery, the introduction of the English principle of equality
before the law, and, above all, an unsettled
vacillating policy, which last has the worst

possible effect upon all the nationalities, European, as well as native, throughout South Africa.

"The present attitude of even British South Africa, is one, not of expectancy, but of slight hope, mingled with distrust, and after such conspicuous events as the dismemberment of Zululand, the retrocession of the Transvaal, in addition to the ineffective efforts towards confederation, he would be a bold man who, as an Englishman, would dare assert either that his country protected her children, or her dependent races, or that there is any settled British policy in the very Continent, where vigour, firmness, and consistency, combined with mere justice, seem to be absolutely essential.

"South Africa has yet to be won over to England, or, in other words, confidence has to be restored. The effort is surely worth making, and anything like a determined effort on the part of the Sovereign, and Her Majesty's immediate advisers would find a most vigorous and cordial response.

" The idea of confederation seems to be quite dependent upon such preliminaries, as mutual confidence, and a measure of common necessity, in order to such a question being seriously entertained.

" The Colonial Conference of two years ago, seems however to have paved the way for effective development in the direction of confederation.

" For it must be remembered, that the somewhat complex British constitution is not the creation of any one Monarch, or Parliament. It has grown to its present dimensions little by little, influenced always by the necessities of particular cases. The House of Peers has ever been summoned by writ, and early precedents indicate, that the Sovereign was not always limited to a particular class of Barons, who alone could be invited to the deliberations of the nation.

"Although it is not admitted, it is nevertheless the fact, that, at the present time, all who are most anxiously desirous of seeing a way to establish a means of drawing together, in Council, the Colonies and the Mother Country, are quite disagreed, as to what is the best means to this end.

"A formal confederation is desired, but all are agreed upon the difficulties which, for the present, at any rate, stand in the way of completing an exactly defined treaty, or definition, to confederate as between the Mother Country, and the Colonies.

"Perhaps a means to this much-desired end may be discovered, by way of less formal, but almost equally effective, courses of policy as regards Colonial possessions.

" Every one feels the difficulty in the way of summoning Colonial Representatives to either the House of Lords or the House of Commons, for, while special provision would be required to increase the numbers of the House of Commons, there are apparent and real obstacles in the way of inviting Colonial Representatives to sit in the House of Lords, either as ordinary, or as *Life* Peers.

" It does not seem too much to hope that, before long, the Crown, may desire to see assembled in London, during some period of the annual session of the Imperial Parliament a Council of Colonial Delegates, meeting in a place to be assigned to them, who will have no voice in other than Colonial Policy, just as now, the House of Lords has no voice in the originating of Money Bills, who will be free to discuss any measure affecting Colonial Policy in general, or the affairs of any Colony, in particular, who will be entitled to forward their conclusions, requests, or opinions to Her Majesty's Principal Secretary of State for the Colonies, and who will constitute a most effective means for ascertaining the current of opinion in any particular Colony for the time being.

" The Houses of Convocation might be referred to as an example of an extra Parliamentary Body of recognised position in the deliberations of the State.

"And, to revert to South Africa, the sympathies, and probably loyal adhesion of all the intelligent classes of every nationality, would be elicited by nothing more than by the express personal interest of the Sovereign, and Her family in the Cape Colony. The occasion of the visit of Prince Alfred, when a mere child, elicited unbounded demonstrations of enthusiastic loyalty to the Crown, and those from Dutch and English alike. The name " Alfred," in

honour of His Royal Highness, is to be everywhere met with in connection with all sorts
of public bodies, Volunteer Corps, and other
Institutions.

" Personal influence goes for more than all
the defined policies of successive administrations,
or excellent theories of Government. A Prince
is of more weight than the best of official
Governors, and it is not likely that in medieval
ages, or even at later periods, such an appanage
of the Crown, as we desire South Africa to
become, would be unvisited by either the
Sovereign, or someone of the Sovereign's family.
The visit of their Royal Highnesses Prince
Albert Victor, and Prince George of Wales
was limited to a brief sojourn at Cape
Town, and did not extend to the Colony in
general.

" The necessity for the employment, in the
interests of the Empire, to use the phrase most

practical,—uncouth, however, it may seem,—of our Royal Princes appears to be a very decided and certain means to the end we have in view, namely, the binding together, by means of sympathetic enthusiasm, the Colonies to the Mother Country, but most particularly the creating of a healthy common accord between South Africa and Great Britain.

" Let any Colony or Dependency feel assured that it is regarded as worthy of attention by those nearest to the Crown, and any sense of isolation, any suspicion that the people, or their country are regarded with any measure of contemptuous indifference must forthwith vanish. Sympathy, encouragement, personal contact, seem to be essential elements to the solution of what is admittedly a problem."

I regard this letter of my well informed correspondent as a most interesting and truthful expression of wide-spread opinion.

s

among the intelligent classes of Her Majesty's loyal subjects in South Africa.

I do not believe the South African political problem to be insoluble. Two things are required to solve it satisfactorily. For the present,—I quote the eloquent words of a distinguished politician with whose wise and noble sentiments I cordially agree—" what we ought to do in a case of this kind is to send out a statesman of the first order of talent, patience, and truthfulness, irrespective of politics or prejudice. For it is an Imperial problem of the highest importance ; and the powers of true patriotism and ambition should be amply gratified in dealing with it."

And for the future, let me add my own earnest conviction, that what is wanted is Imperial Federation, as the goal to be ultimately reached, to render South Africa politically satisfied and content.

Imperial Federation means a constitutional system, under which she would be no longer misruled and misunderstood, by a Government, in which she has no share, in which she places no confidence, and by whom her wants and wishes are often ignored. It is not, as is frequently untruly asserted by writers, and speakers, who have neither studied, comprehended, nor understood its theory and intention, its end and aim, that it means the subjugation of the independence of the Colonies to the control of the Mother Country.

As one of its most earnest advocates, I emphatically protest against all such erroneous interpretations, as a libel on the principle put forward, as a plan for the National Government. On the contrary, the project of Imperial Federation, without any *arriere pensée*, clearly and distinctly involves the condition, that the Colonies themselves are to take their adequate part, and share with the Mother Country in its future concrete constitution. In the brief, but expressive phrase, I have already publicly adopted, Imperial Federation means, "the Government of the Empire by the Empire." In Imperial Federation, therefore, South Africa would be fairly and influentially represented, along with the other Colonies of Great Britain. In union with them she would take her part in guiding the policy, and directing the destinies of the whole British Empire.

APPENDIX I.

THE following discussion took place on the paper read by Sir Frederick Young, on South Africa, at the opening meeting of the Session of the Royal Colonial Institute, on November 12th, at which the Marquis of Lorne presided :—

PROFESSOR H. G. SEELEY: In common with you all, I have listened with great pleasure to this interesting and wide-reaching address. I have not myself been so far afield. My observations were limited to Cape Colony; and the things which I saw in that Colony were necessarily, to a large extent, different from those recorded by Sir Frederick Young. On landing at Cape Town I naturally turned to what the people of South Africa were doing for themselves, and confess I was amazed when I saw the great docks, by means of which the commerce of South Africa is being encouraged, and by which it will hereafter be developed. I was impressed, too, with the educational institutions, the great Public Library, worthy of any town, the South African Museum, the

South African College, and the various efforts made to bring the newest and best knowledge home to the people. But perhaps in Cape Town, the thing which impressed me as most curious was the new dock, in process of construction by excavating stone for the breakwater and other purposes. This work was carried on by coloured convict labour. The convicts thus become trained in useful manual work, as well as in habits of obedience, and when they are discharged, are not only better men, but people in whose work employers of labour have confidence. I learned that the great public mountain roads in Cape Colony have thus been constructed by convict labour, at a comparatively small cost, while the convict acquires skill and useful training. Going up country, my attention, among other matters, was turned to the distribution of mineral wealth and difficulties of water supply, for, as Sir Frederick Young has remarked, the water supply is one of the great problems which all persons have to consider in South Africa. The season during which rain falls is short, and the rain drains rapidly down comparatively steep inclined surfaces, so that science of many kinds has to be enlisted to conserve the water, and turn the supply to account. I found the rocks of much of the country have been curiously compressed and hardened and thrown into parallel irregular folds, and that these rocks were afterwards worn down by the action of water, at a time when the land was still beneath the ocean, with the result that many basin-shaped depressions are preserved and exposed, each of which holds a certain amount of water. Just as we never dream of putting down a well in this country without knowing the positions of the water-bearing strata, so it is hopeless to bore profitably for water in the Colony till the districts are defined over which the water-bearing basins are spread. Nothing arrests the escape of water in its course through the rocks more efficiently than intrusive sheets of igneous rock which rise to the surface, but until the distribution of these dykes is systematically recorded it will not be possible to open out all the water which is preserved underground. There is no doubt that by utilising geological facts of this nature, a better water supply may be obtained, which will enable more land to be brought under cultivation, and larger crops to be raised. I may say that the Colonial Government is fully aware of the importance of following out such lines of work, and steps are being taken to give effect to such exploration. Vegetation, however, by its radiating power, must always be one of the chief aids to improved water supply. In the matter of mineral wealth, Cape Colony is not so rich as some adjacent lands. It contains coal, but the individual beds of coal are thin, and owing to this thinness the coal necessarily alternates with shale, which is more conspicuous than in the coal fields of Britain. I remember that Professor Sedgwick, my old master in geology, told me that in his youth seams of coal only some four to six inches thick were worked on the sides of hills in Yorkshire, and that the coal was carried on horseback over the country to supply the wants of the mountain population. Cape Colony is in a far better state than that. In the Eastern Province the beds of coal are frequently a foot or two or more in thickness. They crop out on the surface with a slight dip near to the railway, and although only worked at present in a few pits (as at Cyphergat, Fairview, Molteno—I did not visit the Indwe)—the coal-bearing rocks certainly extend over a much wider area of country than that which has been explored. One of the happy results at which I arrived in my short visit to this district was to find that there are certain extinct forms of reptilian life associated with these coal beds, by means of which the geological horizon upon which the coal occurs may be traced through the country; so that there is a prospect of this mineral being followed along its outcrop in the Eastern Province with comparative ease by this means. It is desirable on all accounts that coal should be burned rather than timber, since the destruction of wood is harmful to the supply of water. With regard to the gold of Cape Colony, I have not the requisite knowledge to speak with the same confidence. The quantity in any district is probably small: the amount is great in the aggregate, but very widely diffused. Gold appears to be present in small amounts in almost all the volcanic rocks, so that as those rocks decay and new mineral substances are formed out of the decomposed products, the gold which they contained is often preserved and concentrated in thin and narrow veins of zeolitic minerals, which extend over the surface of these volcanic rocks. To what extent these zeolites may be hereafter worked with profit it is impossible at present to say, for much may depend upon water supply, by means of which the ore would be crushed and washed, and much on the varying quantities of gold present in samples from different localities. On the whole, the utilisation of science in the service of man, especially in relation to metals, coal, and water supply, if systematically carried out, will, I believe, be an element of future prosperity to Cape Colony, and enable the Colony to minister to the welfare of adjacent lands.

Mr. J. X. MERRIMAN: I am sure South Africans are very grateful indeed to the amiable and kindly critic in the person of Sir Frederick Young. It is no new thing to Colonists to owe him a debt. All those present will acknowledge the great things he has done for the Colonies in connection with the Royal Colonial Institute. Sir Frederick Young is a man who has been content to look after small things, and the result is this Institute has been worked up by the individual efforts of Colonists and others to its present flourishing condition. I hope the Institute will long flourish, and never be absorbed by anything under more magnificent auspices— in other words, that you will "paddle your own canoe." It is good sometimes to have a plain statement from a plain man. South Africa suffers under a plague of experts who, after spending a few weeks there, tell us exactly what we ought to do; and we don't like it. I wish I could speak to you as a sort of amiable critic, but I have the misfortune to belong to that much-despised class the local politician, and I notice that, when anybody says anything about the Colonies in England, all unite in kicking the local politician. In order not to sail under false colours, I state frankly that I belong to that class. Of course, South Africa is creating a deal of interest at the present time. People who come to fortunes usually do excite a great deal of interest among relations who may in times gone by have given them the cold shoulder. There can be no doubt as to the material prosperity of South Africa at the present time, and still less doubt as to the future. The gold fields of Witwatersrand are unique in the world. This is not my own statement, but the statement of eminent mining engineers from America. For thirty miles and more you have a continuous stretch of reef, which gives throughout a uniform yield per ton, and which has been proved to the depth of some hundred feet, and may—there is every reason to believe—go to unknown depths. The reefs are now being worked in the most economical manner. When proper appliances for mining are used, and when we get the stock-jobbers off our backs, I believe a career of prosperity will open of which few people dream. From another point of view, to those who love the country and make their home there, there cannot but be a seamy side to the picture. Great wealth brings other things in its train. It has brought into South Africa a great spirit of gambling. People neglect the honest industries of the country: they leave their farm work, and rush off to make

T

fortunes in a minute. Everybody—from the king to the beggar—
is gambling in gold shares. Everybody neglects his business, and
talks about nothing else. I ask whether this is a wholesome state
of society? Is it not a state of society to which we may look with
some degree of apprehension? I believe myself that things will
work round, but, undoubtedly, the state of affairs is serious. After
all, there is something which goes to build up a country besides
material wealth, and I am not sure that gambling in gold shares
is exactly the thing which is wanted. Of course, there have been
other countries where these vast increases of material wealth have
occurred—California and Australia—but there the conditions were
different. They were new countries, which attracted large numbers
of white men, and, when they found the gold fields did not pay,
they made homes for themselves on the land. Unfortunately, that
state of affairs does not exist at the present time in South Africa,
and that brings us face to face with the great problem on which
Sir Frederick Young has touched—the great problem which we have
always before us—viz., how two races utterly alien to each other,
the black and the white, are to live and increase side by side.
South Africa is the only country in the world where that problem
exists, excepting the Southern States of North America. This is a
great question, on which the future of South Africa depends.
Unfortunately, the white men do not work in a country where the
black race flourishes. If the white man does not become a "boss,"
he sinks to the level of a mean white man. The difficulty is to
get a state of society in which the white race shall flourish side
by side with the black; and when people talk about the "local
politicians," the "average Cape politician," and the like, they
should remember we have to deal with this enormous problem—
that we are anxious to do justice to the "black," and at the same
time we are naturally anxious to see the European population

flourish. I believe the gold fields will attract a large European population. The wages are enormous. There are 20,000 black men, without a stitch upon them, earning as much as eighteen shillings a week a-piece, and getting as much food as they can eat, in the mines of Johannesburg. People talk about the treatment of the blacks. Nobody dares to treat them badly, because they would run away. There is a competition for them, and the black man has an uncommonly rosy time of it. The white men naturally wont work under the same conditions as the blacks. I saw a letter from an operative cautioning his fellow artisans against going out. He says, "We get thirty shillings a day, but it is a dreadful place to live in." I ask the operatives in England to mistrust that statement. ("What is the cost of living?") You can live at the club very well indeed for £10 a month the club, mind you, where the aristocracy live. It is idle to tell me the honest artisan cannot live. In addition to the black and white population, there is another problem, and that is, the influx of Arabs, who creep down the East Coast through the door of Natal. They are gradually ousting the English retail trader. You may go to up-country towns, and in whole streets you will see these yellow fellows, sitting there in their muslin dresses, where formerly there were English traders. In places where we want to cultivate the English population, that is a very serious thing. Our yellow friends come under the garb of British subjects from Bombay, and are making nests in the Transvaal and elsewhere by ousting the English retail trader. Sir Frederick Young has alluded to State colonisation. I am sorry to differ from so amiable a critic of our ways, but, as one who has had a little experience, I can tell him that you may send Colonists out, but you cannot as easily make them stay there. If they make their fortunes, they come home to England to spend them. If they are poor, and bad

times come, the black man crowds them out, and off they go to
Australia. You can depend on a German peasant settling, but
bring an Englishman or a Scotchman, and he wants to better
himself. In that he is quite right, but he does not see his way on
a small plot of ground, and off he goes down a mine, or something of that sort. There are great difficulties in the way of
State-aided emigration. We do not want the riff-raff; we don't
want the "surplus population." It is one of the greatest difficulties to get decent, steady Englishmen to settle on the land.
It is the people who settle on the land who make a country, and
if Sir Frederick Young can give us a receipt for making English
people settle there he will confer one of the greatest possible
benefits on South Africa. Sir Frederick Young departed from the
usual custom on such occasions by touching on politics. I am
glad he did, because more interest is given to the discussion, and
there is nothing like good, healthy controversy. Sir Frederick
Young is greatly concerned that there should be a settled policy
for South Africa. All I can say is, in Heaven's name, don't listen
to a syren voice of that kind. So surely as you have a settled
policy—some great and grand scheme—so surely will follow
disaster and disgrace. The people of South Africa may be very
stupid, but they are very much like other people—determined to
make their policy themselves, and the policy of South Africa is
not going to be framed in Downing Street. I cannot help thinking
Sir Frederick Young did injustice to some of my friends who have
been at the head of affairs. "The mournful mismanagement of
South African affairs," he says, "during the last twenty-five years,
and most especially during the last decade, has been truly lamentable, and cannot fail to awaken the saddest feelings on the part
of every loyal Briton and true-hearted patriot." But have affairs
been mismanaged for the last twenty-five years? The revenue

twenty-five years ago was £500,000. It is now nearly £4,000,000. For twenty-five years, under the beneficent rule of Downing Street, we had not a mile of railway. Now we have 2,000 miles. Twenty-five years ago there was no national feeling at all. Now there is a strong South African feeling, which is destined to grow and build up a South African policy. As to the talk about a settled and firm policy, Sir Philip Wodehouse was the last Governor who had a grand scheme from Downing Street. A more honest, conscientious, and able man did not exist; but his policy was a failure. Then came my friend Sir Henry Barkly. His policy was distinctly opposite. It was a true policy for South Africa. It was a policy of *laissez-faire*. The result was, things went on as merrily as a marriage bell, Dutch and English drew together, the natives were quiet, South Africa was prosperous, and everything went on as happily as possible till Mr. Froude and Lord Carnarvon hit on the grand scheme of uniting South Africa. From that day our misfortunes began. One of the most able, courteous, and high-minded gentlemen in the British service—Sir Bartle Frere—was sent to carry out this firm policy. What was the result? Failure. I will say nothing more about it. Then Sir Hercules Robinson reverted to the *laissez-faire* policy. South Africa was under a shade—nobody would look at us. But now we are gradually righting ourselves, and getting into a prosperous condition. Now are being raised again the cries for a grand policy. I caution you against them. Let us manage our own affairs. *Laissez faire, laissez aller*—that is our policy for South Africa. There are no nostrums required. The one thing required is the gradual bringing of the Dutch and English together. There are no two races more fitted to unite. You know how like they are to Englishmen. The Boer is as like the English farmer as possible. There are no people more fond of manly sports than the Dutch; they enter into them heartily, and in the cricket and football fields they are among the best players. They are as fond of riding and shooting as Englishmen are. In fact, the Dutch and the English are as like as Heaven can make them, and the only thing that keeps them apart is man's prejudice. The one thing to do is to bring them together. How can you help that end? Not by girding at them, and writing against Boer ways, but by recognising the fact that they have been pioneers in South Africa, and that they are the only people who will settle on the land. I see there is a great agitation about Swaziland, which is entirely surrounded by the Transvaal Republic. ("No.") Well, except as to Tongaland, and I am not going to say anything about that. The cry is got up, "Don't hand it over to the Boers." In whose interest is that cry got up? It is in the interest of a few speculators, and not in the interest of the capitalists, who have £108,000,000 invested in the Transvaal, and yet are not afraid to trust the Boers with Swaziland. This girding at the Dutch is resented, and does incalculable harm. People at home have very little idea how much influence public opinion in England has in South Africa. Sir Frederick Young has alluded to President Kruger, who won't put down prize fights because he might be thought to be oppressing the Englishman! All I ask is, don't let your talk about union with the Dutch be mere lip service. Trust them ; work hand in hand with them. Unless you do you will make little progress in South Africa. By that I mean political progress. The material progress of South Africa is now secured; therefore my advice is—cultivate the Dutch, because, unless they are our friends, we shall be a divided people, and our black and yellow brethren will get the best of us. Our true policy is, *Laissez faire, laissez aller.*

Sir G. BADEN-POWELL, K.C.M.G., M.P.: My friend, Mr. Merriman, has made a speech of the utmost value to South Africa, and it is

a very fitting, I will not say reply, but comment, on the address
to which we have listened with such pleasure; but Mr. Merriman,
with his strong arguments and apt illustrations, came at the end
to the conclusion at which Sir Frederick Young had arrived. I
have not much to add, but I think we have heard from Sir
Frederick Young a view of South African affairs on the political
side which, I may tell you frankly, differs diametrically from my
own. I have heard from Mr. Merriman a view of affairs in which
I cordially concur, but from neither have I heard of that third
aspect which, I think, is necessary to complete the view. Sir
Frederick Young has told us that for twenty-five years, certainly
during the last ten years, South Africa has been mismanaged. I
must confess I was sorry to hear the strong language he used,
because one cannot but remember that for the greater part of the
last twenty years most of the affairs of South Africa have been in
the hands of free self-governing communities. Cape Colony has
been under Responsible Government since 1873, and the Free State
and the Transvaal have always been self-governing. I agree with
Mr. Merriman that for the last twenty-five years affairs in South
Africa have progressed, with one signal and fatal exception, and
that was the policy under which we took over and then gave back
the Transvaal. Omitting that, I think we have but little to be
sorry for in the history of South Africa. There have been troubles,
but I, for one, think that all difficulties would have been avoided
if the phrase " Imperial aid " had been substituted for that of
" Imperial interference " in the affairs of South Africa. It is the
aid which has been given by the Mother Country which has
resulted in developing the material resources, and, above all, in
establishing the security from native attack of various European
States in South Africa. Sir Frederick Young spoke of the attitude
towards the Imperial Government. I could wish he had been in

Cape Town on the day Sir Charles Warren landed, and seen the ovation he received from all classes. Let me add this—that the Bechuanaland expedition, which was led by Sir Charles Warren, and in which I had the good fortune to take part, cost the Mother Country perhaps £1,500,000, but in the discussions in Parliament or in the press as to the future of Bechuanaland, the fact is seldom mentioned that Bechuanaland was acquired for the Empire at the cost of the British taxpayer. Let me remind you of another fact, which the Cape Colonist well knows—that when the Imperial Government wished, from wise motives of economy, to extend the Cape system of railways to Kimberley, at a time when the Cape Ministers were not prepared to carry out the extension, the British Parliament advanced a loan of £400,000, at a low rate of interest, for that object. Another instance I could quote, in connection with the history of that interesting native territory—Basutoland. You remember how that country was handed over to the Cape Colonists, and that for various reasons the management of the Basutos got beyond their power, the result being that the Imperial Government went to the aid of the Cape Colony and took back Basutoland. I mention these cases because they illustrate an aspect of affairs which is, I think, apt to be neglected. We at home—and certainly those who have enjoyed the kind hospitality of their brethren in South Africa—wish to do all we can to aid our fellow-countrymen in that part of the globe. We do not wish to interfere, and I should like to see this put forward as the grand and final policy of South Africa—that we are ready to aid that portion of the Empire, but set our faces against interference. In conclusion, I will add that I am sure all of us congratulate Sir Frederick Young on having so successfully accomplished his arduous journey, returning to us, as he does, in better health than when he left. If you wish to renew your youth, and grow younger instead of older, follow his example—make a trip through South Africa, sleeping in the open veldt.

Dr. SYMES THOMPSON: Another year's experience has confirmed and strengthened my conclusions as to the remarkable salubrity of the South African climate in cases of chest disease and of nerve wear, which I laid before the Royal Colonial Institute in November last.   While regarding the neighbourhood of Cape Town and Grahamstown as beneficial for a short sojourn, among the upland stations I would call attention to Middelburg and Tarkestad. Hotel accommodation and adequate comfort for invalids, as regards food, quarters, attention, occupation, and amusement, are still most deficient.   During the recent drought the dust storms proved very trying to the eyes and to the bronchial membranes at Kimberley, and at Johannesburg the dangers were great.   I rejoice to learn that Sir Frederick Young has found his winter trip so health-giving, and believe that a similar expedition might prove of immense value to many Englishmen who are overwrought in body or in mind.

The CHAIRMAN (the Right Hon. the Marquis of Lorne, K.T., G.C.M.G.): I propose a hearty vote of thanks to Sir Frederick Young for his kindness in reading the Paper.   I was extremely interested myself, as I think you all were.   In his political observations, and in speaking of a firm policy, I think that, after all, what the reader of the Paper meant was firmness in allowing each nationality to develop itself as it best might, with aid from home. I think that is the sense of his observations, and I am sure we are obliged to him, not only for speaking of more personal matters, but also for telling us the actual impressions he derived from the journey.   I entirely agree with Mr. Merriman—and I believe Sir Frederick Young does—that, finding ourselves in South Africa with the Dutch, we must work with them and through them.   I hope

U

the Dutch will allow themselves to be helped in one matter which Sir Frederick Young impressed on President Kruger—apparently not with great results—viz., in the matter of railways, and that they will allow railways to pierce the Transvaal. I am sure he is a man of too much intelligence very much to object to railways. That policy would be too much like that of the Chinese. I remember, when I was at the head of a society in London, asking the representative of China to come and listen to a paper in regard to railways through Siam. He said solemnly—"Chinese not like railways." I said this railway would not go through the Imperial dominions—that it would only be at a respectful distance. Again my remarks were interpreted to him, and again, after a long pause, he solemnly replied—"Chinese don't like railways near frontier." I am sure President Kruger will not fritter chances away in that manner, and that he will allow us to help him.

SIR FREDERICK YOUNG, K.C.M.G.: I feel extremely flattered by the compliment which our noble Chairman has been good enough to pay me. It was really most gratifying to me to be able to take the interesting and instructive tour from which I have recently returned, and the only difficulty and hesitation I felt as to giving an account of what I saw was that I saw so much that I did not know how I could crowd a tithe of it in the reasonable dimensions of a paper. I was a little in dread, I confess, when so astute and able a politician as Mr. Merriman rose to make his criticisms; but I wish him to understand, as well as you, that the view I put forward—perhaps I did not explain myself as clearly as I ought to have done—was that advocated by Mr. Merriman himself, namely, that South Africa should be allowed to frame her own policy. That is the sum and substance of what I wished to say on that point. As the noble Marquis has been so kind as to act as my interpreter, I need not take up more of your time by enlarging on this question. I have now the greatest possible pleasure in asking you to join with me in thanking the noble Marquis for having, as one of our Vice-Presidents, been so kind as to preside on this occasion.

APPENDIX II.

IMPERIAL FEDERATION.

An address on the above interesting subject was delivered by Sir Frederick Young, K.C.M.G., in the Y.M.C. Association Hall, on Monday, when the room was filled to its utmost capacity. The chair was taken by the President of the Association, Mr. E. J. Earp, who, in introducing the lecturer to the audience, said he was a gentleman who was well and favourably known to many colonists, who had received great attention and kindness from him during their visits to the Old Country. Sir Frederick Young had very kindly responded to the invitation of the committee to lecture this evening, and though the subject of Imperial Federation was of a somewhat political nature, still it was not of such a character as to preclude its being spoken about within the walls of the association. The subject of the lecture was one worthy of all attention, which had recently been occupying the attention of eminent statesmen of various political opinions. This was an age of specialists, and he thought that Sir Frederick Young might be well considered as a specialist on the subject upon which he was now about to address them. He had for many years been connected with the Royal Colonial Institute, and his services had received recognition at the hands of his Sovereign.

SIR FREDERICK YOUNG, who was most warmly received, said in the first place he must tender his hearty thanks to the Chairman for the very kind manner in which he had introduced him. The attention of the audience this evening would be directed to the desirability of promoting the unity of the British Empire. Before commencing his address, he wished to emphasize what the Chairman had already expressed with regard to the rules of the association on political subjects. In connection with that, he would say that the subject he was about to speak upon did not touch upon party politics in any way, as it was a National question, and might be excepted from their rigid rule. The subject of Imperial Federation was, to his mind, of so vast and vital a character, and of such importance to the whole nation collectively, that it impressed him with the responsibility he incurred in speaking upon it, and the feeling he had of being unable to do full justice to it. He spoke with some confidence on the subject, because he claimed to be one of the pioneers of the idea of Imperial Federation, which meant "the government of the Empire by the Empire." He wished to take his hearers back to the origin of English parliaments, when the first idea of representation occurred to our early kings, and when the scattered portions of England were at last drawn into one focus of representation by Edward III., and gradually that kind of representation succeeded in effecting the Union of England and Scotland, and subsequently Ireland, things remaining in that form until the present day. Latterly, our Colonial Empire had grown up to wonderful and vast dimensions, but as far as the principle of representation was concerned there had been no great change, though it was perfectly true that during the past few years a certain number of the Colonies had obtained what was called self-government, or what he called the shadow of English government on the parliamentary system, as retained in its original principle and plan up to our own times. The Imperial policy of the British Empire was entirely conducted at Home, and Imperial Federation meant that this system should be changed, and that those who were living outside the borders of the British Isles should have their true participation in the government of the Empire. This led him to a point on which there was very much misunderstanding on the part of those who had heard the subject of Imperial Federation mentioned, and who thought there must be some idea of those who advocated it at Home getting some advantage over their colonial brethren, and draw them into a net, by which they would have to part with their rights of local self-government. He utterly denied that there were any such intentions —on the contrary, this was an invitation to them, a cry from the Old Country, asking them to come and assist in governing the Empire. This could only be effected by Imperial Federation, which would mean the termination of what was called the rule of Downing Street, which would be superseded by something far different, and, in his opinion, be far more acceptable to the colonists themselves. They would not have to suffer, as they had in the past, in many ways, from ignorance, prejudice, and narrow views, but they would have an opportunity of taking part in the policy of the Empire, particularly in that which affected themselves. In consequence of the agitation at Home during the past few years a successful attempt had been made to establish what was called the Imperial Federation League, of which he was an active member, and which took no part in party politics, and was at the present moment presided over by Lord Rosebery, with the Hon. E. Stanhope, the present Minister of War, as Vice-President, who, so far as party politics were concerned, were on totally different sides. That would prove that in England they did not regard this great question as one of party politics. One of the most important results in connection with that League had been the celebrated Colonial Conference, which the League had been able to induce the Government to summon two years ago at Westminster. They all knew what a remarkable gathering that was, which was presided over by Lord Knutsford (then Sir Henry Holland), the summons being responded to by the self-governing Colonies of the Empire sending their foremost men to represent their interests. From South Africa were sent such men as Sir Thomas Upington, Sir John Robinson, and Mr. Hofmeyr, and he confessed that, when he had the honour of being at the first meeting of the Conference, and seeing these men gathered in the Foreign Office, and having present the Prime Minister, Lord Salisbury, if his dream of Imperial Federation was to be anything more than a dream, he felt that these were the first symptoms of its realization. It was the first time in history that the Colonies of Great Britain had come to the Mother Country to consult on great National questions. He had read nearly the whole of the large Blue Book which contained the reports of the Conference, and all he could say was that he challenged any assembly of public men to meet together and show more ability and statesmanlike thought in the discussion of the questions submitted to them than was shown by that Conference during its short reign. He was delighted with the noble words of Lord Salisbury, when he expressed his satisfaction, and said he hoped this would be only the first of many similar Conferences, but Lord Salisbury, like other public men, sometimes saw occasion to change his views, because not long ago he said, on a public occasion, that all he knew about Federation was, that it was a word spelt with ten letters, which was somewhat of a wet blanket to some of those who had reckoned upon Lord Salisbury as an ardent supporter. More recently he said, in reply to a question put to him at a public meeting at the East End of London, that geographical considerations would prevent the realization of such a scheme; but his allusions to geographical difficulties vanished before modern science. Was it not in their cognizance that in South Africa, through the medium of the telegraph, they were able to know what was taking place in England within twenty-four hours? Geographical considerations, indeed! that might have been all very well some years ago, when it took three or four months to reach the Cape, but now it took only two or three weeks, and that time would even be probably reduced as time wore on. Such being the case, geographical considerations had nothing whatever to do with the matter. He had no desire to speak unfairly of the gentleman who occupied the position of Prime Minister of the Empire, but he felt sure the time would come when Lord Salisbury would think that Imperial Federation was something more than a word of ten letters; and that his geographical considerations would vanish also, as having no reason in them. In contrast to Lord Salisbury, he would read a short extract from a speech, made only a few months ago at Leeds by Lord Rosebery, when he said : "For my part, if you will forgive me this little bit of egotism, I can say from the bottom of my heart that it is the dominant passion of my public life. Ever since I traversed those great regions which own the sway of the British Crown outside these islands, I have felt that there was a cause, which merited all the enthusiasm and energy that man could give to it. It is a cause for which any one might be content to live; it is a cause for which, if needs be, any one might be content to die." Lord Rosebery was at this moment the President of the Imperial Federation League, and only recently he addressed a letter, on behalf of the League, to Lord Salisbury, asking that the Government would summon another Conference like the one which took place with such wonderful results two years ago, and which Lord Salisbury had said he hoped would be the first of many more. The answer he gave, however, was something to the effect that he did not think it desirable that the Government should move in the matter, but that the Colonies should take the initiative. With all humility he would ask how anything of this kind could be moved, except by some motor? There must be something to move the colonists, and who could do that so well as Her Majesty's Government, by inviting, in a courteous and sympathetic spirit, the Colonies to come again and consult on Imperial subjects. He would now touch upon some of the errors prevalent on this great question of Imperial Federation. In some of the Colonies, New Zealand in particular, something had been said that in course of time independence must be the inevitable result. But he asked why should this be the case? He would also like to say something about what were Imperial questions? Some of the subjects which would be dealt with by the Imperial Federated Parliament would be those of National defence, peace and war, and all subjects in which national interests are concerned. As he had attempted to explain, it would be a federation in which the Colonies would be completely and fairly represented. The whole subject resolved itself into this: Representation. One hundred years ago, one of our distinguished statesmen in England, Charles James Fox, said that "representation was the sovereign remedy for all evils," and that was what was contended for by Imperial Federation. He would now venture to make some allusion to one of the most distinguished statesmen in South Africa, who attended the Conference in London—he alluded to Mr. Hofmeyr—who made a most re-

W

markable speech. He was sorry it was too long to read, but he would select a portion of that very statesmanlike address. Referring to the fourth and eighth subjects proposed for discussion—viz., the feasibility of promoting a closer union between the various parts of the British Empire by means of an Imperial tariff of Customs, to be levied independently of the duties payable under existing tariffs on goods entering the British Empire from abroad, the revenue derived from such tariffs to be devoted to the general defence of the Empire—he said: "I have taken this matter in hand with two objects, to promote the union of the Empire, and at the same time to obtain revenue for general defence. It would establish a connecting link between the Colonies mutually, as well as between the Colonies, and the Empire also, such as is not at present in existence, and which might fuller develop, by-and-by, into a most powerful bond of union." Again, speaking of how this was to be effected, he said: "A body would be required with legislative, and, to some extent, administrative powers; in other words, you would have a limited fiscal Parliament by the side of the British Parliament and the various Colonial Parliaments. This small body, which would have to be created, would perhaps be the germ of an Imperial Federation afterwards." He thought those were most remarkable, and striking words. If people would think the subject out in a calm judicial, and fair spirit, they would see in it the fulfilment of what would not only promote the best interests of the British Empire, but would also be the handmaiden of civilization to others as well, because in it there was no idea of aggrandisement. He had recently made a most remarkable tour through this interesting country, and since he landed in Cape Town, on the 24th May, had seen a great deal of it. He had visited Kimberley, and gone down in a bucket to see one of the diamond mines; he had travelled to Vryburg, and across the treeless desert in the south-western portion of the Transvaal to Klerksdorp; thence on to Johannesburg and down the gold mines, and further on to Pretoria, where he had an interview with President Kruger, and attended meetings of the Volksraad. He had been 150 miles north of Pretoria, and dwelt for a fortnight in the open veldt, without going near a house, and had seen the Kafirs in their kraals. He had crossed the Transvaal, through Heidelburg and Newcastle, in Natal, down to Durban, he had visited Port Elizabeth and Grahamstown, and had now returned to Cape Town. What he had seen of this great country had astonished him, and he thought it had a vast future before it; but it required to be governed in the most enlightened and satisfactory manner, and he appealed to both races—Dutch and English—to co-operate and unite in developing its wonderful resources. It was by this way alone—by cordial co-operation and a generous feeling towards one another, that this would be realized. He believed that Imperial Federation would be the best solution of the difficulties which had arisen. He had heard whispers of what was called Republicanism. We worshipped words rather than things; but the British Constitution, especially when it would be expanded by Federation, would be practically a Republic with a Queen as President. He would, therefore, appeal once more to the judgment of thoughtful men to weigh the principles contended for, calmly, wisely, and without prejudice or passion. The flippant, the superficial, the thoughtlessly ambitious, and those who did not take a fair, judicial, and comprehensive view of the great issues involved in it to each portion of the Empire over which the British Crown held sway, might deride and condemn it, but he, as one of its most ardent pioneers and supporters, recommended it to all colonists as well as to his countrymen at home, as the best preservation of their commercial, social, and political interests in the future, which they

would lose altogether if they abandoned it in favour of the dis-
integration of the British Empire. He had studied this question
for some years, and by a sort of instinct he felt that it was the
right thing to be brought about. He had brought before them
proofs that some distinguished men were already feeling the
desirability of some such thing being effected, and he could not
but help thinking that their ranks would be augmented by other
people of influence and power, who may hereafter be brought to
think seriously and carefully over this great question. He took
the opportunity himself, some three years ago, to put a letter in
the London *Times* suggesting that as the question had now been
some years before the public, both in the Colonies and the Mother
Country, it would be very desirable indeed if a Royal Commission
of Inquiry were sent out, under distinguished auspices, for the
purpose of ascertaining the opinions of the various Colonies. This
could be carried out on parallel lines to the celebrated Commission
sent to Canada, and which resulted in the consolidation of the
Dominion. The obtaining of these opinions would be invaluable
evidence as to the consensus of feeling in the Colonies on the
subject. If the question was to be more than a dream, and
became one of practical politics, it would require all the Colonies
to express an opinion on the subject. He could not conceive that
anything could be more desirable than to take the evidence of
distinguished representative men on such a great National question.
Those were the views he expressed in the leading journal; they
were individual ideas, which did not yet appear to be acceptable,
though he could not help hoping that the day would arrive when
some such Royal Commission might be appointed, which would
give an impetus to the question—and, at all events, afford all those
who took such a deep interest in it an opportunity of seeing how
far, in the opinion of the various Colonies, such a change in the

British Constitution could be effected, to the entire satisfaction of all concerned. There was no desire on the part of the Mother Country, in propounding questions like this, to take any advantage of the Colonies, or do anything which would not be for their benefit. There was no hurry on the part of the Mother Country. which simply asked the Colonies to help to govern and take part in the National politics of the British Empire.

Mr. J. A. BAM proposed a vote of thanks to Sir Frederick Young for his able and instructive lecture, which was heartily accorded.

SIR FREDERICK YOUNG having acknowledged the compliment, the proceedings closed with a vote of thanks to the President.

GEORGE BEECHING & SON, Printers, Upper Baker Street, London, N.W.

www.ingramcontent.com/pod-product-compliance
Lightning Source LLC
Chambersburg PA
CBHW030535040726
47497CB00008B/2467